MW01124132

Monsters in the Attic

Happy Holidays
To: Rilla Harmony Earth
From: ?
Congratulations!
You have received a gift membership
to the *Monster of the Month Club*

February

March

January

Icicle

Sweetie Pie

Shamrock

M.O.T.M. Club Rules:

1. A new monster selection arrives on the first day of every month.

2. The monsters come from different countries around the globe.

3. Instructions for the care and feeding of each monster are included in every box.

4. Good luck. . . .

DIAN CURTIS REGAN

Monsters
in the Attic

ILLUSTRATIONS BY
LAURA CORNELL

HENRY HOLT AND COMPANY – NEW YORK

Henry Holt and Company, Inc.
Publishers since 1866
115 West 18th Street
New York, New York 10011

Henry Holt is a registered trademark of Henry Holt and Company, Inc.

Library of Congress Cataloging-in-Publication Data
Regan, Dian Curtis. Monsters in the attic / by Dian Curtis Regan.
     p.   cm.
   Sequel to: Monster of the Month Club.
   Summary: The stuffed toy monsters Rilla has been receiving from
the Monster of the Month Club are continuing to come to life, and
she desperately tries to hide them from her mother and aunt.
   [1. Monsters—Fiction. 2. Toys—Fiction.] I. Title.
PZ7.R25854Mr 1995 [Fic]—dc20   95-16174

ISBN 0-8050-3709-8
First Edition—1995

Printed in the United States of America on acid-free paper. ∞

10 9 8 7 6 5 4 3 2 1

For Ginger Knowlton

CONTENTS

Monsters in the Attic

1
NOISES IN THE NIGHT

It happened again.

Rilla Harmony Earth was sound asleep in her attic bedroom at the Harmony House Bed and Breakfast, *smack* in the middle of a dream about her mother and aunt (proprietors of the B & B).

In the dream, they'd sneaked into her attic (which they *never* did) and discovered the cookie tin that held Rilla's most intimate possessions.

Collapsing onto the water bed in hysterics, her aunt (Poppy) and mother (Sparrow) were howling over excerpts from Rilla's journal—the one she'd started the moment Joshua Banks (her one true love) noticed she was alive.

Splash . . . gurgle . . . smack!

The noises burst into Rilla's dream, yanking her awake.

Something is in your bathtub, her groggy mind warned.

Puzzled, Rilla crept from bed, tripping over slippers she didn't need on this muggy May midnight.

With every step closer to the tiny attic bathroom, her heart pounded louder and louder, until *whoever* or *whatever* was splashing in the tub could certainly hear the thunder clapping of her heart.

Should she turn on a light? What if it was a burglar?

In your bathtub?

Oh, right, she said to herself. Dumb.

Could it be one of the B & B guests?

I repeat—in your bathtub?

Dumb again.

Besides, the attic door was locked and the windows didn't open. Whatever had taken over her tub couldn't have broken in from outside.

Which left only one answer.

An answer that turned the *frightened* pounding of Rilla's heart into an *excited* thump-thump-thumping.

She clicked on the bathroom light.

Floating in the tub was a mermaid.

A *monster* mermaid. A mer-monster, if you will.

"Chelsea?" Rilla whispered, fascinated by the sight of a creature with wavy hair the color of seaweed backstroking across her tub with a slow flip-flipping of her shimmery tail.

The mermaid was smaller than Oreo, the mama cat

who lived with her kittens in the barn. Chelsea's abundant green hair was tangled with bits of shells and tiny starfish, and her tail was aqua—a cross between the color of the ocean on a clear day and the eyes of José (a frequent B & B guest).

The mermaid's face was the most humanlike of all the monsters Rilla had received so far from the Monster of the Month Club. Her membership had been a gift from Mr. Tamerow, another B & B guest, whom she loved dearly but who didn't have a clue that the monsters were more than stuffed toys—*much* more.

Cocking one ear, Rilla listened to a faint melody the mermaid sang as she circled the tub in lazy strokes. Was it the kind of music Caribbean sea creatures sang to one another late on moonless nights?

Smack!

Rilla flinched as Chelsea slapped her tail against the surface of the water. Was she hungry? What did monster mermaids eat?

Rilla couldn't remember. She'd have to check the card that had come with the April Selection of the M.O.T.M. Club.

Backing out of the bathroom, Rilla felt her way across the dark bedroom and clicked on a lamp.

The meager glow was just bright enough to light the contents of the bottom dresser drawer as she pulled out a cookie tin—the one Sparrow and Aunt Poppy had invaded in her dream.

Rilla started to fish out the selection card.

Wait! her memory cried.

If Chelsea was "alive," then . . .

Rilla scrambled across her rumpled water bed to the chair where her stuffed animal collection spent their nights. In the dim light, her eyes searched for a silver monster with a poofy tail, seven eyes, and tiny fangs.

"Icicle," Rilla crooned, "there you are." She lifted him from the pile. He'd been the first monster to arrive. The January Selection.

The thrill of seeing him "real" again quickly turned to disappointment. He was nothing more than a "cozy collectible," as the monsters were called.

Icicle was a grumpy pain in the toe; don't you remember?

"I know, I know," Rilla whispered. Still, she missed Icicle for some strange reason, even though he was here with her. Sort of.

"Sweetie Pie?" she called, finding the February Selection buried under Abraham, the polar bear. (Named after Mr. Tamerow, who'd brought him from Alaska.)

Sweetie Pie was as stiff and still as Icicle. So was Shamrock, the March Selection, who'd never come to life at all.

Her curiosity sadly satisfied, Rilla climbed across the bed, smoothing the honeycomb-patterned quilt before lifting the monster cards from the cookie tin. She sorted them until she found the one she was looking for:

> *Monster of the Month Club*
> ───────────
> April Selection
> *Name:* Chelsea   *Gender:* Female
> *Homeland:* Aruba
> *Likes:* Kelp, salt water, tuna
> Do not keep out of water too long

Rilla chuckled at the instructions. She hadn't put Chelsea in water at all, even though her sleek vinyl "skin" was probably waterproof. It was the mermaid's hair, full and curly, that Rilla didn't want to ruin.

She'd set Chelsea on the shelf next to the tub—which explained how the mermaid had turned on the water faucets to create her own home.

"Kelp, salt water, and tuna," Rilla read out loud, yawning. "The kitchen is three floors down; she'll have to wait until morning."

Why is Chelsea swimming in your tub? Rilla's mind asked. *Yet Icicle, Sweetie Pie, and Shamrock are still stuffed and silent?*

The question promised to keep her awake, and it was already half-past midnight, according to her bedside clock. The "magic" must have been sparked at twelve o'clock sharp.

Maybe the Legend of the Global Monsters held the

cryptic answer. Rilla dug through papers in the cookie tin until she found it:

Once, when stranger things than monsters roamed the earth, these tiny creatures shared nature with us, living in small colonies scattered throughout the world. Belief held that spotting a mini-monster in the wild meant good fortune would follow for a year.

Today, likenesses of the monsters have been created as cozy collectibles. Yet, legend warns, when stars line up in angled shapes like lightning, real monsters tread the earth once more.

Ms. Noir, the librarian, had given her a book on astronomy. Rilla had been shocked to discover that the monster legend was based on a real scientific occurrence. According to *Funky Facts About Stars*, lightning-shaped star patterns randomly appeared over different countries at various times of the year.

So. That must explain why Chelsea, from Aruba, was "alive," yet Icicle, Sweetie Pie, and Shamrock (from Botswana, New Zealand, and Ireland) were not.

As Rilla packed the cards back into the cookie tin, anxiety began its wild dance in her stomach.

Why?

Part of her was fired up about another live monster in her attic. Yet part of her remembered how much trouble the others had been. Keeping them a secret. Keeping them fed. Keeping them quiet. Until the night the stars shifted, breaking their lightning pattern—and breaking the magic.

How long would Chelsea stay? Rilla wondered. At least the mermaid could remain in the tub while *she* used the shower stall.

Unable to resist another peek, Rilla tiptoed back into the bathroom.

This time, Chelsea acknowledged her. Hooking tiny arms over the side of the tub, she lifted her upper body out of the water.

"Hello," Rilla said, gingerly touching the mermaid's wet arm.

Chelsea gibbered a monster hello. Shoving off, she did a few loop-de-loops, as if wanting to impress Rilla.

Sitting on the towel hamper, Rilla applauded the mermaid's underwater antics until the girl's eyes grew heavy and she couldn't stop yawning.

In spite of the "bathtub miracle," she desperately needed to get back into bed. Sparrow home-schooled her, so being late to school wasn't a problem. The problem was that tomorrow—or rather, later this morning—she was meeting with the other six home-schoolers for final exams before summer vacation.

How could she concentrate on finals when a monster mermaid was swimming in her bathtub?

Bidding Chelsea good night, she clicked off the light

and hurried back to bed. Too bad she had to keep such a wonderful creature a secret. But if Sparrow—and the world—found out, well, forget it. The monsters would be taken from her to benefit science and tabloid TV. Zoos and carnivals.

Rilla would *never* let that happen.

She closed her eyes. Soft splashing noises lulled her back to sleep.

Ka-thunka-thunka-thunk.

Rilla yanked a pillow over her head to block the *other* noises. The muffled thumpings coming from the closet.

Muffled thumpings? Coming from the closet?

Ka-thunka-thunka-thunk.

She shot out of bed. A pillow and a stuffed pig flew off into the darkness.

Something was in her closet.

Something she'd totally forgotten about: the *May* Selection of the Monster of the Month Club . . .

2
MONSTER IN THE CLOSET

Rilla's heart zipped back to its panic thumping.

In the mist of midnight confusion, she couldn't even *remember* the May monster.

Clicking on the light again, she dove for the cookie tin, shuffling cards until she found the proper one:

Monster of the Month Club
———
May Selection

Name: Burly   *Gender:* Male

Homeland: Argentina

Likes: Baseball cards, Cracker Jacks, golf tees

Doesn't like to lose

Oh, right. The May monster was a sports fanatic.
Ka-thunka-thunka-thunk.

Rilla stole to the closet and opened the door.

Burly stopped what he was doing to blink at her in the lamplight. What he was doing was bouncing a tennis ball against a wall of the closet.

The monster's fur was the same color as the lumpy oatmeal Sparrow forced on Rilla on cold winter mornings. His face resembled a baby bear's.

He was dressed in a red-and-navy rugby shirt, shorts, socks, and athletic shoes. A whistle hung on a red ribbon around his neck, and a baseball cap perched backward on his head, with holes cut out for bear ears.

He seemed annoyed at the interruption.

Rilla remembered the collection of mini-balls that had come with the May monster—soccer, football, baseball, and basketball. Should she give him one of those to play with?

Not unless you want him to bounce it against the wall.

Groan. The last thing she wanted to do was disturb B & B guests—the number one no-no at Harmony House.

Burly rubbed his tummy.

Ah, the universal monster sign for hunger.

"You'll have to wait until morning," Rilla told him. "Sorry."

The monster's fuzzy eyebrows dipped into a scowl. He gave the tennis ball an angry toss. *Ka-THUNKA.*

It bounced off the wall and boomeranged into the room.

Rilla caught it with one hand.

Uh-oh. He wants to eat, and he wants to eat NOW.

"Give me a second," she told him. Moving a chair to the closet, she climbed up to reach the top shelf, pulling down an old shoe box marked in black crayon with a giant **3**.

Thank heavens she liked to keep things. Aunt Poppy called her a pack rat of the worst kind.

Rilla dumped the contents of the box onto her desk and peered at the messy pile. These were things saved from her third-grade class at Pickering, the school she attended before Sparrow began home-schooling her.

She and Kelly Tonario (one of the home-schoolers) used to collect and trade baseball cards because Kelly's big brother traded cards with his friends, but he wouldn't let her join them.

Rilla hoped her collection wasn't valuable because the cards were about to become monster food.

Burly climbed onto the desk to watch. Rilla selected a Barry Bonds card, then shoved everything else back into the box. "Sorry, Barry," she muttered, tearing his card into tiny pieces.

Before she could finish, the impatient monster snatched the card from her hands and began to gnaw on one corner.

How hungry was he? Rilla chose a Ken Griffey, Jr., and left it on the desk, then stored the box back on the closet shelf.

By the time she'd climbed into bed, Burly was nibbling the Ken card. Uh-oh. Her stash would have to last until she could get to Mr. Baca's One-Stop Shoppette to buy more, plus Cracker Jacks and golf tees.

Mermaid food might be easier to find. Salt water was simple to make. Tuna? Surely Sparrow had tuna in the pantry for B & B guests. And kelp? Kelp was one of the herbs Sparrow took daily, so that wasn't a problem.

The *problem* was—how could she round up mermonster food before the home-schoolers arrived? She'd already set the alarm for five thirty so she could get up early and cram for tests. (She still didn't have all the trace minerals memorized, and Sparrow was big on trace minerals.)

Another reason for getting up extra early was to work on the new hairstyle she wanted to wear for Joshua Banks (her one true love).

She'd seen the hairdo in *Sassy:* a side ponytail, woven through with tiny braids, clasped at the ends with nifty beads she and Marcia Ruiz (another home-schooler) had found at a hobby shop.

Did she have time to cram, do her hair, *and* find monster food before eight? She'd have to hustle.

Sighing, Rilla blinked to make sure she wasn't imagining the sight before her: a stuffed animal, hunched on top of her desk, gnawing on a baseball card. "Go to sleep," she told him.

As if he understood, the sports monster jumped to the

floor and headed back into the closet, trailing pieces of Ken Griffey, Jr., from each hand.

Again Rilla clicked off the lamp and closed her eyes to sleep. Yet one last worry kept her dreams at bay.

May was almost over.

June would be here soon.

A new month meant a new monster. That's how the Monster of the Month Club worked.

How could she sleep knowing the June Selection was winging its way from some far corner of the earth to Harmony House Bed and Breakfast to join her and Chelsea and Burly?

And to make her life terribly, terribly confusing.

3

AUNT POPPY'S PRIZE

The five-o'clock alarm jangled much too soon, inter-rupting a different dream—a jumbled one about undersea soccer games, with monster players and mer-maid cheerleaders, whose shouts of "Go, team! Feed me!" rose to the surface in tiny bubbles.

Moaning, Rilla stretched. The night before finals was *not* a good night for a monster crisis.

Pulling herself from bed, she moved quietly to her desk. Better let sleeping monsters lie. She had work to do.

"Cramming" notes waited on her desk, sprinkled with bits of baseball cards. The sight assured her that her midnight adventure wasn't a nightmare wrought by too much end-of-the-year review.

Math she was good at. English. Her grade would be based on an essay. (She hoped her topic wasn't *List and Discuss All Sixty Trace Minerals.*)

Science. She'd already completed a project for her grade—four anemometers to measure wind speed around the B & B's yard. She'd designed them from paper cups, wooden dowels, and hobby-store meters.

That left social studies, art history, and health. Three areas needing more than an hour's worth of cramming.

Sighing, Rilla opened her health notebook, ready to attack those pesky trace minerals. But every time she got to cobalt, monster noises reminded her she had two hungry creatures to feed and hair to braid.

"Forget it." Flipping the notebook shut, she headed for the shower.

Chelsea was floating on her back, tail motionless.

Rilla touched her.

Startled, the mermaid came to life. With a wiggle of her tail, she dove under, searching for a place to hide.

Too bad there were no hiding places at the bottom of Chelsea's "sea."

Why not? Rilla's mind asked. In the shower, she plotted how to turn the tub into the Caribbean Sea surrounding Aruba. A few rocks, a little greenery. How hard could it be?

Rilla dressed, then swept her wet hair into a side ponytail. After forty minutes of fumbling and fussing with braids and beads, she grimaced into the mirror at her lopsided hairdo—*not* the way it looked in the magazine.

Chelsea had a lot of advice to offer. In monster jabber.

Forget what the mermaid thinks. Will Joshua like it? Will Tina?

Tina Welter was the one home-schooler Rilla could live without. The girl loved catching the Earth family doing something weird. Of course, Aunt Poppy and Sparrow gave her lots of opportunities.

Rilla stuck out her tongue at her reflection, then went to check on Burly—who was being awfully quiet. She found him asleep in the closet, clutching her tennis racket like a teddy bear.

Hoping both monsters stayed quiet, Rilla tiptoed out, locking the door with a key on a silver chain around her neck.

The third floor consisted of single suites and was decorated in blue, with moon-and-stars wallpaper. Aunt Poppy had dubbed it the blue floor.

Another flight of stairs brought Rilla to the family suites on the green floor (green-herb patterned wallpaper and carpet).

A polished oak banister curved to the main floor's entry hall. Sparrow's antique rolltop desk served as the registration desk (inherited from Great-grandfather Knox and shipped to the B & B from Austria).

Next to the desk sat a sideboard, covered with brochures of local tourist attractions. A large dining room bordered one side of the entry hall and a parlor for guests bordered the other.

Right now, the double oak front doors were wide

open, spilling morning sunshine across the parquet floor. Two men in dark overalls struggled to steer a huge contraption through the entry hall.

Rilla paused on the stairway. What was going on?

A barefooted Aunt Poppy flitted about, directing the men toward the parlor. A bathrobe was thrown over her jeans, and her waist length hair was wet, as if the delivery truck had interrupted her shower.

"Morning!" she hollered up to Rilla. "My prize has arrived."

"Prize?" Rilla scrunched her face at the odd machine.

Aunt Poppy loved entering sweepstakes. She'd won things before, but never anything this big and ugly. Her prizes were always useless—like a year's supply of barbecue sauce (for a family of vegetarians?) and an accordion, which she'd desperately tried to play, with José the musician's help. Rilla (and Sparrow) had been greatly relieved when Aunt Poppy gave up and turned the accordion into a parlor decoration.

"What *is* it?" Rilla asked, watching the deliverymen.

Aunt Poppy's eyes appeared over the top of the instruction manual. "My weight machine."

"You're going to lift weights?" Somehow Rilla never pictured her aunt as a weight lifter.

"Mm-mmm." Aunt Poppy kept reading while the men dumped extra straps, pulleys, cables, and springs in the middle of the parlor, then left.

"What's all the commotion?"

Sparrow, spatula in hand, stood in the doorway. A smudge of seven-grain Belgian-waffle batter was smeared across one cheek.

Her eyebrows flew up as she took in the weight machine. "That . . . that *atrocity*," she sputtered, "can*not* stay in my parlor."

"Just for now," Aunt Poppy reassured her. "Until I get it assembled and figure it all out."

Sparrow wrinkled her nose. "You're going to *keep* it?"

"Of course I'm going to keep it."

"Why?"

Aunt Poppy regarded her big sister as though she'd asked why honeybees made honey. "I need to get into shape." She slapped a hand on each hip. "*Some* of us care about how we look because we *might* be in the market for a new husband."

Rilla snickered. Aunt Poppy never missed a chance to comment on her big sister's "healthy hips" (what Sparrow called them).

Sparrow aimed the spatula at her sister. "How many husbands does one need? Isn't four enough?"

Rilla covered her mouth to keep from laughing out loud.

Aunt Poppy absorbed the snide remark. "With *your* track record for husbands, maybe *you* should give my *atrocity* a try."

Rilla gasped. Aunt Poppy had gone too far. The topic

of Sparrow's husband, a.k.a. Rilla's father, was taboo at Harmony House—at least when Rilla was in earshot. He'd left before she was born so Rilla never knew him. Now she had a zillion questions, but never asked them for fear of what the answers might be.

Good time to clear out.

Skirting the sisters—now locked in a glaring contest—Rilla hustled to the kitchen for monster food: one can of tuna, Sparrow's bottle of kelp, a water glass, a box of Celtic sea salt, and a long-handled spoon.

That took care of Chelsea.

With her armload, Rilla hurried up the back steps (the servants' stairway in the old days) to the attic.

She hoped the baseball cards would satisfy Burly until she could go monster food shopping.

Right now, she needed her full concentration for final exams—or she'd be the only home-schooler who didn't pass.

How humiliating *that* would be.

4

SIDESHOW IN THE PARLOR

Humiliation took on a whole new meaning when the home-schoolers arrived. Mrs. Welter (Tina's mom) came first, shuttling Tina, Marcia Ruiz, and Andrew Hogan in a mini-van.

Greeting them at the door, Rilla tried to hurry them to the area beside the kitchen that served as her classroom. But the iron abomination looming in the parlor was too hard to ignore.

Swooping around Rilla as though she were invisible, the home-schoolers made a beeline toward the machine.

"I can't believe anyone would *buy* one of these things."

That came from Mrs. Welter as she tapped her manicured nails on the padded bench. "I mean, isn't it easier to go to a spa?"

Rilla couldn't imagine Mrs. Welter as anything but the "exercise-lite" type, with her perfect hair and coordinated clothes.

"Only the Earths would own something this obnoxious."

That came from Tina, who shared her mom's talent for matching accessories but whose spiky hair and bitten-off nails ended the similarity.

Marcia flipped her dark braid over one shoulder and giggled at Tina. Then, shooting Rilla an apologetic look, she pretended a sudden interest in Aunt Poppy's accordion, now arranged on a table with candles and seashells.

Andrew snatched up the instruction manual while Mrs. Welter straddled the leather bench.

A dried and dressed Aunt Poppy burst into the parlor. "Isn't it groovy?" she gushed, helping Tina's mom position the weight against her shoulders. "It was second prize in the Pump for Your Health Sweepstakes."

Rilla cringed. First because *nobody* said "groovy," and second because of her aunt's weight-lifting garb. She'd donned baggy sweats and a T-shirt with a picture of a rabbit in dark glasses holding a white cane. Underneath were the words: LAB ANIMALS NEVER HAVE A NICE DAY.

It was all fuel for the fire that kept Tina Welter convinced the Earth family was weird, weird, weird.

While Aunt Poppy traded places with Mrs. Welter to offer a demonstration, Wally Penguin arrived. His real last name was Pennington, but nobody called him that. His generous nose had spawned the nickname.

Next came bubbly Kelly Tonario.

And Joshua Banks.

Rilla had hoped the sideshow in the parlor would be over before her one true love appeared.

"Hi, Earth," Joshua said, his grin dipping into dimples on both sides of his cheeks. "Are you ready for this?"

Rilla's smile faltered. Did *THIS* mean

1. His arrival?

2. The convulsions his arrival was giving her heart?

3. Aunt Poppy and her Pump for Your Health prize?

4. Final exams?

5. The last day of school?

"Sure." Her bland response covered all possible meanings.

"Nice hair," Tina jeered.

Had Tina been waiting for Joshua to arrive before commenting on the braids and beads? *Figures.* Rilla glowered at her.

"Where *is* everybody?" Sparrow stepped into the

parlor, scowling at the sight of Aunt Poppy, flat on her back, with the home-schoolers cheering her attempts to bench-press fifty pounds.

Rilla snickered. Had her mother hoped to find them holding a last-minute review session of major geological formations of North America?

Sparrow quickly herded everyone back to the classroom.

The area had once been living quarters for domestic help. Now maps and posters decorated the walls, making it a cheery place to work. The room was filled with tables, a computer, an aquarium, and cages of "borrowed" animals. (Sparrow didn't believe in keeping caged animals, so four-legged visitors were borrowed and returned—or freed.)

Rilla loved the room, but she preferred meeting at someone else's home in a corner of the kitchen or basement, like at Wally's, instead of worrying what her bird-mother or flower-aunt might do to embarrass her.

Especially in front of Joshua.

Normally refreshments were served when they met, but today snacks would come after finals—which was just as well, since no one gobbled down Sparrow's amaranth-banana flan the way they did Mrs. Tonario's chocolate-raspberry twirls.

In a sudden flurry of activity, tables were spaced apart, pencils sharpened, notebooks slammed and stashed—and nerves began to frazzle.

Along with a bad case of exam stress, Rilla battled a lump in her throat. Other than Tina, no one had mentioned her hair. Not even Sparrow.

Did it look ridiculous? Why had she bothered . . . ?

Mrs. Welter (miffed, because she'd chipped a nail on the weight machine) gave instructions while Sparrow handed out test papers.

Quiet filled the room.

Rilla's stomach rumbled.

Hunger wasn't conducive to test taking, but she'd barely had time for a bite of Kashi after dashing to the attic to serve kelp-topped tuna and a glass of sea-salted water to the tub monster.

Burly had woken and climbed to the top shelf of her closet, dumping out boxes until he'd found Rilla's stash of baseball cards. Not much she could do about the mess until later. (She'd pieced together a half-eaten card to see who it was. Tony Gwynn . . . good-bye, Tony.)

Forcing monsters from her mind, Rilla squinted at a math equation, trying to concentrate. The only sounds in the classroom were scribbling pencils, shuffling pages, occasional coughing, and . . .

Ka-thunka-thunka-thunk.

A confused Mrs. Welter circled the room, glancing out each window, trying to locate the source of the annoying noise.

A puzzled Sparrow stepped into the hallway to listen.

Distracted home-schoolers fidgeted.

Ka-thunka-thunka-thunk.

Rilla's heart skittered.

Faint, rhythmic thumping could have many sources.

But the most *logical* source was a hungry sports monster playing soccer in the attic.

5
BUMPINGS AND THUMPINGS

"Psst!"

Rilla ignored glares from Tina and Andrew. It was her mother's attention she wanted—not theirs.

Sparrow tiptoed to Rilla's table. "Are you stuck on a problem?"

"No. I, um, know what's causing that, um, thumping noise."

"You do?" Sparrow tilted her head, pulling off her wire glasses as if it would make her hear better. "I figured it was one of the B & B guests."

Groan. Rilla could have kicked herself. Of *course* Sparrow would suspect a guest. How simple.

"So what is it?" Her mother mouthed the words to keep from disturbing other test takers.

Rilla bit her lip, wishing she could reel in her words. Now it was too late to say, "Oh, nothing."

"Earth to Earth." Sparrow tapped her shoulder. "You called me over here. So, tell me what's bumping and thumping, and I'll go stop it."

"No!" Sending her mother was *not* what she had in mind.

The home-schoolers lifted their heads to stare at her.

Sparrow's face mirrored their puzzled expressions. "What's *wrong?*"

"*I* will stop the noise." Rilla scrambled from her chair.

"Wait!" Sparrow hissed, trying to keep her voice low. "You can't leave in the middle of a test." She grabbed for Rilla's sleeve but missed.

Ignoring the murmurs, Rilla was out the door, through the kitchen, and up the back steps before Sparrow could catch her.

Tearing to the attic, she fumbled for the key, bursting through the door just as Burly drop-kicked a football.

Rilla lunged, intercepting the ball before it *ka-thunka*'d against the wall—stopping another bumping and thumping cold.

With a happy chitter, Burly dove for her legs.

Rilla crumpled to the floor. "You *tackled* me!" she yelped.

Burly looked at her, as if saying, "That's what I'm supposed to do."

Rilla stood, dusting herself off. "I'm *not* playing football with you."

Circling the room, she collected every monster ball in sight, plus two tennis balls and a tiny rubber ball from her jacks collection.

"Now what?" she mumbled, searching for a spot to hide them. No place in the attic was safe from monster paws.

Rilla shifted her armload. "I can't take these downstairs; they'd think I was crazy."

That left only one solution.

Slipping into the bathroom, she tiptoed past a sleeping tub monster, opened the bottom cabinet, and dropped the balls, one by one, down the laundry chute. Four stories.

Rilla hoped Aunt Poppy wasn't in the basement doing laundry. Balls raining from above would surely spark a few angry questions.

The instant she closed the cabinet, Burly confronted her, paws on chubby hips, prattling furiously in monster talk.

"You'll have to find something *else* to do," Rilla told him.

What? she asked herself. *He's a sports monster. Sports monsters play ball. What else do you want him to do?*

Rilla resisted an urge to lock Burly in the ball-free closet. Too mean.

"Hey, *I* know." Leading him to the dresser, she clicked on her radio, twirling the dial until she found the twenty-four-hour sports station. A show called *Jock Talk* was on.

Burly's eyes sparked in recognition of phrases like "batting average," "RBIs," and "turning a double play." Scrambling onto the bed, he joined Rilla's stuffed animal collection, settling in with the pillow creatures to listen.

Rilla adjusted the volume as low as possible. "I'll play ball with you later," she promised. "Stay here and be quiet."

An overwhelming urge to pat Burly's fuzzy cheek and kiss his forehead took hold of her. So she did.

Burly made a chortling noise that sounded an awful lot like a purring kitten.

It gave a sentimental twist to Rilla's heart.

Tearing downstairs, she breezed into the classroom and slid into her chair, pretending she hadn't just broken a home-schooler rule.

Six pairs of eyes threatened to burn holes through her.

"If I left the room during a test," Tina muttered, "I'd be *flunked*."

"Would you care to explain?" Sparrow asked.

Rilla crooked a finger, motioning her mother closer.

"No." Sparrow leaned against a table and crossed her arms. "I think we'd *all* like to hear your excuse for breaking our strictest rule."

Rilla's insides dissolved into molten lava. Was Sparrow going to make her confess? In front of everyone? How could she be so cruel?

"I was trying to *help*," she snipped, hearing her voice quiver. Did they think she left to consult a hidden cheat sheet?

"Go on," Sparrow urged.

At that moment, Rilla truly disliked her mother. *Why can't she ever defend me?*

"Well," Rilla began, nervously crinkling one corner of her test paper. "I, um . . . forgot to turn off that toy the family from Cincinnati left behind. It kept running into the wall. Over and over."

Quick thinking, Earth, she told herself. The Cincinnati family and their seven children had stayed at Harmony House last week. When they checked out, they left a whole slew of things—a baby bottle, two books, and a wind-up toy. Wouldn't have surprised Rilla if they'd left a kid or two.

Yet she didn't want to say she'd been playing with the Cincinnati kids' toy—especially in front of the homeschoolers. Rilla glared at her mother, who'd accepted the explanation with a disgusted shrug.

Tina was snickering. She winked at Joshua Banks.

Winked! At Joshua. Because of Rilla's lameness.

The nerve.

Shoving her emotions deep inside, Rilla opened a blue book to begin her English essay. Topic: *Promoting Harmony in Our Day-to-Day Lives.*

Rilla bore down on her pencil with a heavy hand.

Boy, did *she* have a lot to say on the topic of harmony, starting with a list of suggestions for her own dear mother.

Thank heavens summer vacation was only a few long hours away.

6
SCHOOL'S OUT

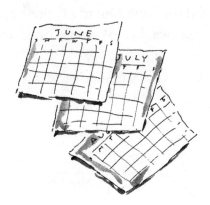

"Good-bye!" Marcia called, dashing for Mrs. Welter's van.

Kelly raced off in another direction. "Have a fun summer, everybody!"

"No more pencils, no more books, no more teachers'—" Andrew and Wally swallowed the rest of the ditty as they burst out the front door and came face to face with Mrs. Welter.

"Thanks, kids," she said, playfully *thwacking* them on the shoulders.

Rilla stepped onto the veranda to wave good-bye, which was silly since the home-schoolers lived in the same neighborhood and were bound to run into each other all summer.

Joshua breezed past. "Bye, Earth." He jabbed a thumb toward her hair. "Cool braids."

HE NOTICED! Rilla grinned, shrugging as if it were no big deal.

"See you around this summer?" Joshua asked.

Around? Rilla gazed into his brown-and-gold-speckled eyes. She wanted to say, "Define *around*. Is it a place? Do you want to meet me there on a certain day at a certain time?"

He was waiting for an answer.

"Sure," she replied, light and friendly. "See you around, too." She emphasized the word to give it special meaning—just for the two of them.

Joshua leaped off the side of the porch.

Tina whizzed by, bumping Rilla's shoulder—accidentally on purpose. "Want a ride home, Josh?"

Josh? Now she's calling him by a cutesy nickname?

"No thanks. Got my bike." Joshua pulled it from the azalea bushes and ran toward the driveway, hopping onto the seat in one swift movement.

Rilla gloated. Joshua could have put his bike in the back of Mrs. Welter's van and ridden home with Tina. But he didn't want to.

After everyone left, the sudden quiet was refreshing. Rilla lingered on the veranda, breathing in azalea-laced air and smiling at the blue sky. This was her favorite time of year. And the promise of twelve whole weeks of freedom made her feel absolutely giddy.

Duty tugged her back inside. It was time for the

mother of the monsters to make a midday check on her children.

"Where are you going?"

Rilla stopped on the stairs to peer down at Sparrow. "School's out," she reminded her teacher-mother.

"Not quite. We still have to talk about your summer project. After that, you can eat lunch and have the whole afternoon to yourself."

Rilla collapsed dramatically, sprawling across five steps.

Sparrow rolled her eyes. "What's that supposed to mean? Remember last summer? You had fun working on your project."

Rilla lifted her head. Sparrow wasn't going to fall for her melodrama.

"Meet me in the classroom and we'll discuss this year's assignment."

"Rats." Rilla rolled out of the way of guests tromping down the stairs.

Last summer *had* been fun, she admitted, volunteering at the library, helping Ms. Noir, who'd let her do everything—reshelve books, enter new titles in the computer, and plan story time.

Her favorite part of the job was reading to a roomful of children. She'd learned how to use different voices to make the kids hang on to every word.

Rilla rose to her feet. Better not keep Sparrow waiting.

At the bottom of the stairs, grunting noises drew her

attention to the parlor. Aunt Poppy was still pumping iron. Now she had an audience of B & B guests *oh*ing and *ah*ing her amazing strength. She was quite entertaining.

"Rill!" Sparrow hollered from the classroom.

Her mother had as much patience as Burly.

Rilla obliged, feeling grumpy. "There ought to be a law against assignments on the last day of school," she muttered.

Back in the classroom, she reached for an untouched plate of carob kisses left over from this morning. The cookies wouldn't go to waste—they'd be recycled to the guests' dinner table, as well as the Earths'.

"Since you enjoyed working with books last summer," Sparrow began, riffling through a notebook, "your assignment for this year will be . . ." She flipped a sheet of paper onto the table in front of Rilla.

Rilla read it out loud. "Write a book?" She gaped at her mother. "You want me to write a book during my summer vacation?"

"Mm-mmm. Doesn't have to be a novel, mind you. Remember the toddler books you read for story time at the library?"

"Oh, the short ones." Rilla felt relieved.

"The other parents and I came up with topics for everyone."

"You mean the other home-schoolers have to do this too?"

"Of course."

Somehow *that* made her feel a whole lot better.

"The topic I've chosen for you is . . . herbal remedies."

"Wow, what a surprise." Rilla acted shocked. "Imagine Sparrow Harmony Earth picking an *herbal* topic for her Earth daughter."

Sparrow looked as if she'd expected such a remark. "You always poke fun at me and my remedies—until you get sick. When my concoctions make you feel better, I don't hear you complaining."

Rilla shrugged. Sparrow's strange brews *did* work. Still, it seemed weird having a mother who mixed potions like a wizard instead of handing out aspirin, like everyone else's mother.

"Remember the time we got you over the flu in forty-eight hours so you could be in the Christmas play at Pickering?"

"Yes." It was true; she couldn't argue.

"You can include other home remedies besides herbs, if you like." Sparrow closed her notebook. "That's it. School's out—for both of us." She looked as happy as the home-schoolers as they'd dashed away from Harmony House.

"Have a fun summer," her mom added. "And by the way . . . I really like your braids and beads." With that, she hurried from the room.

Rilla absorbed the unexpected compliment.

Wandering around the classroom, she stopped at the aquarium to feed the glimmery neon tropical fish (whom she'd secretly named Joshua). Opening a new box of food, she accidentally sliced her finger on a sharp edge.

"Ouch." Rilla stuck her finger in her mouth, sprinkling fish food with her other hand. The cut wasn't deep, but it was bleeding. *I'm already doing research for my book—ha.*

Rilla studied her finger. "Chapter One," she murmured to Joshua (the fish). "'Herbal Remedies for Cuts and Scrapes' . . ."

7

A SURPRISE GUEST

Rilla planned to check on the monsters, then attack Sparrow's mountain of natural-healing books to find a remedy for cut fingers.

But when she got to the attic, Burly was moping around, looking pathetic as he searched for the monster balls—and food?

The radio was still on. Rilla guessed he wasn't interested in the current program: *Let's Bowl!*

No time now for curing cut fingers. Rilla grabbed a simple Band-Aid, then hurried downstairs to retrieve the monster's balls from the basement.

They were wet. Aunt Poppy had accidentally washed them along with the load of towels they'd fallen into.

Uh-oh. Now seemed a good time to disappear from Harmony House and go monster-food shopping.

After reuniting the balls with their relieved owner,

Rilla rode her bike to Mr. Baca's One-Stop Shoppette. She cruised every aisle but could not find golf tees. Cracker Jacks she found, as well as more baseball cards (on sale!) in case she needed them. But no tees.

"Excuse me." Rilla tapped Carlos, Mr. Baca's son, on the shoulder as he knelt to stock a lower shelf with Candy Crunchies breakfast cereal.

"Well, hello, Miss Earth," Carlos said. His braces glinted in the light as he smiled up at her.

He was old for braces, Rilla thought. He had to be at least nineteen.

But they never kept him from smiling.

Carlos offered her a cereal box the color of strawberry cotton candy. "Are you looking for breakfast cereal?"

They both laughed. *She* knew that *he* knew Sparrow would never allow something called Candy Crunchies within throwing distance of Harmony House.

"Yeah, right." Rilla shoved the box away, secretly wondering what the pink crunchies tasted like. "Do you sell golf tees?"

"Are you taking up golf this summer?"

No, I'm feeding tees to my pet monster. Out loud, she answered, "Maybe."

"You'll have to try Soozi's Sporting Goods. Sorry."

Rilla paid for her purchases—including one chocolate mint. Its chewy sweetness was heaven after those horrid carob kisses.

Next she rode her bike to the sporting-goods store, where Soozi herself, wearing a rugby outfit remarkably similar to Burly's, escorted her to the golf department.

"What else do you need?" Soozi asked. "We have golf shoes, golf clubs, golf balls, golf towels, and golf hats— all on sale today."

Rilla waved a box of yellow tees. "This is all, thank you."

Soozi aimed her toward a cashier. "When you get home, be sure to tell your father about our huge golf sale."

Rilla tried to answer, but the mention of her father tapped the ol' instant anger that boiled inside her whenever she thought of him.

Paying for the tees, she hurried out to her bike.

"Do you play golf?" she snootily asked her invisible father, shoving the tees into a bag with the other monster food. Such a simple question. Most kids would know the answer. Not Rilla Harmony Earth—whom her father had known as Rilla Pinowski.

No, that wasn't true. He hadn't known her at all. He left before she was born. Back when Sparrow was Donna and Aunt Poppy was Aunt Sally.

Why did Soozi assume the golf tees were for her father, anyway? Wasn't that sexist? They *could've* been for her mom or aunt.

Or for me, she thought

The fact that golf tees were food for the May monster was just as hard to believe as the fact that her father didn't care where—or *who*—she was.

What made her even angrier was that Sparrow never mentioned him to her own daughter—the one who had the right to know.

Slinging the shopping bag over her bike's handlebars, Rilla pedaled as fast as she could until the anger she felt toward her father *and* mother burned up in her frenzied ride.

Tearing down Hollyhock Road, Rilla hit the brakes to navigate the sharp turn past the evergreen hedge into Harmony House's drive.

A yellow taxi was backing out.

SCRI-I-I-I-I-TCH!

CLUNK-BUMP!

That was the sound of Rilla's bike skidding on the gravel, clunking against the cab's bumper, and knocking her—forehead first—against the trunk.

She landed hard. The bike came to rest in a bed of petunias.

The driver leaped from her cab. "Are you all right?"

She dashed to Rilla's side. "The hedge blocked my view; I didn't see you." The young woman held Rilla down by the shoulders as if planning to give her mouth-to-mouth resuscitation.

Rilla twisted out of the cabbie's grasp. "I'm fine," she rasped, although she wasn't certain she was fine until she inspected herself.

Nothing hurt too badly. Her shorts were ripped, and both knees were scraped and bleeding. Touching the bump on her forehead, her fingers came away with a trace of blood.

"Let me help you into the house," the driver said, pulling Rilla to her feet while trying not to get blood on her uniform.

"Really, I'm okay." Rilla's first thought was to inspect her bike and make sure it—and the bag of monster food—had survived the crash.

Her second thought was—who just arrived in the taxi?

"Was your passenger a man?" Rilla asked. "A man who talks a lot and wears funny clothes?"

Oh, please, let it be Mr. Tamerow. He was her favorite B & B guest, almost like a member of the Earth family.

The driver chuckled as she lifted Rilla's bike out of the flower bed. "Yes, my passenger talked a lot and wore funny clothes—only it wasn't a man." The cabbie shook her head in amazement. "It was a woman dressed head to toe in royal blue. And she told me the strangest thing. She said I'd soon live near the sea in a tall, thin house."

Something about the driver's description filled Rilla with dread.

"And her prediction is absolutely true because my boyfriend proposed to me last night. He just got a job overseeing a lighthouse at the tip of Cape Cod. Isn't that amazing? A tall, thin house. Near the sea."

Although Rilla's mind was dulled by the crash, it was still sharp enough to put two and two together. If the B & B's newest guest was a talkative woman who wore blue and told the future—it could be only one person.

A person whose arrival was more painful than sliding across the gravel drive on bare legs.

"Rilla!"

Sparrow was jumping up and down on the veranda, flapping an apron above her head like a warning flag. "You'll never guess who just surprised us with a visit!"

The woman in question stepped onto the veranda behind Sparrow. Holding a hand to shade her eyes, she peered suspiciously across the lawn toward the scene of the accident—and Rilla.

"Ohmigosh."

Suddenly all of Rilla's scrapes and scratches, bumps and bruises began to hurt big-time. Even her braids ached.

"It's true," Rilla whisper-groaned. "Mother Lapis Lazuli has finally come."

8
ANGST IN THE ATTIC

Rilla thanked the cab driver for her concern and wished her a happy life in the lighthouse on the cape.

Rolling her bike off the lawn and up the drive, she avoided eye contact with the B & B's surprise guest, who, in Rilla's opinion, was as welcome as a mailbox full of people-eating monsters.

Rilla, how rude.

Funny how the voice inside her head sometimes sounded more like Sparrow's voice than hers.

Sparrow freaked when she saw the blood. "What happened?" she cried, dashing off the veranda to meet Rilla halfway.

"She took a spill," Mother Lazuli called in a disinterested voice.

Rilla glared at the woman for her lack of sympathy, but the scowl went unnoticed. Mother Lazuli had turned her back to pluck a few azalea blossoms drooping onto the veranda.

The fiftyish woman was beyond plump. Hair the color of steel fell to her waist from a (blue) clasp at the nape of her neck. Steel was a good word to describe her eyes, too. And the warmth of her heart . . .

Mother L.'s dress was large and shapeless. More like a tent. Its deep shade of royal blue was what her name meant.

Lapis Lazuli wasn't her real moniker any more than Sparrow Harmony Earth was her mother's real name. The decision to identify herself with a gemstone had something to do with the power of the rock and the energy of its rich color.

Rilla groaned. Was Harmony House becoming a magnet for weirdos?

Sparrow fussed over Rilla, making sure her bumps and scratches weren't serious. "Good thing we have a doctor in the house," she quipped.

Mother Lazuli was a homeopathic doctor, meaning she was just as gung ho about herbal healing as Sparrow. She was also Sparrow's mentor from her youth. Plus she possessed the gift of Sight, which is how she'd predicted the cab driver's future—and what made Rilla afraid of her.

Who wanted to be around someone who could read minds?

She doesn't mind-read, Earth; she predicts your future.

I'm not so sure. . . .

Sparrow marched Rilla up the veranda steps. "Mother, did you *know* this was going to happen?"

"Puh," the woman scoffed in a voice as deep and throaty as Mr. Tamerow's. "Of course I knew."

"Why didn't you warn me?" Sparrow's voice was soft and questioning.

"Why didn't you warn *me*?" Rilla's voice was irritated and accusing.

Sparrow nudged her to hush up.

Mother Lazuli narrowed sapphire-rimmed eyes at Rilla. "I knew she wouldn't be badly injured. Mishaps often serve as good life lessons. In the future, your daughter will refrain from flying into blind driveways on her bicycle. One hopes."

Mother L. was big on "life lessons."

Rilla followed them to the kitchen. Her mother made her sit on the counter the way she used to when Rilla was a little girl. Then Sparrow cleaned her knees with a soapy cloth and doused them with tea tree oil.

Even though Rilla liked being fussed over, the smell of tea tree oil made her gag. She covered her nose with both hands, listening as Mother Lazuli traded ointment secrets with Sparrow.

Maybe she should be taking notes for her herbal remedy book. *Remember tea tree oil,* she told herself.

"Mother is talking to you," Sparrow said, flicking Rilla on the leg.

The woman was staring at her oozing forehead with such heated intensity, Rilla swore she felt the bloody spot shrivel into a dry scab.

"I'm feeling distress in your daughter's life," Mother L. said.

Sparrow laughed.

Rilla was appalled at her mother's reaction. "You think it's funny?"

She taped cotton gauze onto Rilla's knees. "Mother, my little girl is a teenager now. *Distress* is her middle name."

"Very amusing," Rilla muttered as the two mothers had a good laugh at her expense.

"Well, then," Mother Lazuli said, placing two fingers against her right temple. "I'm picking up angst in the attic."

Rilla felt color drain from her face. If anyone could sniff out monsters inside Harmony House, Mother L. could.

Sparrow patted the last bandage into place. "So, Rill, is there something in the attic I should know about?"

Think fast, Earth. "Um, my book." She hopped off the counter and fiddled with the torn flap on her shorts. "I have to write a book for my summer project," she explained to Mother L. "I'm having trouble beginning."

"Ah." The woman looked deep into Rilla's eyes.

She knows you're lying. That's why she said "Ah."

"Beginnings are always difficult," Mother Lazuli

said. "Whether it's a book, a friendship, a letter, a job, or . . . or life. Once you begin, it gets easier."

Sparrow cleared her throat. Loudly.

"Oh," Rilla said. "Thank you, Mother." The woman charged big bucks for her mystic counseling, so whenever she offered free advice, she was to be thanked, according to Sparrow.

Addressing the psychic as Mother made Rilla uncomfortable. Why couldn't she call *Sparrow* Mother instead of some almost stranger?

She already knew the answer. Sparrow wouldn't allow it because she wanted *Daughter to see Mother as Equal and not Authority Figure.*

So why did Sparrow called Lapis Lazuli *Mother*?

Because she is an authority figure, Rilla's mind answered.

"Can I go now?"

"Wait, I have to do something about your forehead."

Rilla felt her bump. Now it was crusty. Maybe she could comb bangs over it until it healed.

She stood still, holding her nose while Sparrow doused her forehead with the dreaded tea tree oil.

"Better give her feverfew," Mother Lazuli advised.

"Exactly what I was thinking," Sparrow answered.

"Wrong." Rilla let sarcasm seep into her words. "I don't have a fever; I have a bump." *Mother L. made a mistake. Ha!*

The woman glowered at her with a controlled power

that threatened to shrivel Rilla's insides. "Feverfew will lessen the headache that comes with such an injury."

Sparrow handed her two tanned capsules. "Mother is right. Your head is bound to hurt after the blow it received. These will help."

While she talked, she poured hot water into a mug that read:

Let food be your medicine
and medicine be your food.

—Hippocrates

Sparrow fetched several bags of loose herbs from the pantry and sprinkled a bit of each into a tea ball. "Take the capsules with this cup of healing tea."

"Eww, what's in it?" Rilla wrinkled her nose. Tiny green flakes had escaped from the tea strainer and were floating suspiciously in the water. How could she avoid swallowing them?

"I would guess," Mother L. began, squinting at the ceiling. "Valerian, mistletoe, skullcap, and . . . maybe hops. With a bit of chamomile."

"Excellent," Sparrow exclaimed.

How'd she know? Rilla glanced at the ceiling to see if the names of the mystery herbs were written there.

"I also added lady's slipper," Sparrow said. "Herbs to relax the nerves and body after a trauma." She bobbed the tea ball a few times, then removed it and handed the mug to her daughter.

Rilla sipped the tea to make sure it wasn't too hot, then swallowed the feverfew capsules while avoiding Mother Know-It-All's eyes. Herbs for a trauma—ha. She felt more trauma over the blue woman's arrival than she did over her bike accident. What herbs should she take for that?

"Now can I go, please?"

"You may," Sparrow answered, correcting her grammar.

Rilla hated it when her mother played teacher after hours.

"And," Sparrow teased, "please try to avoid oncoming cars."

"More like backing taxis," Rilla mumbled.

Pain was beginning to settle in her knees, so she limped to the front yard to rescue the bag of monster food from her bike's handlebars. Sounds of crunching gravel drew her attention to the drive.

Now who was arriving?

An orange van. On the side were fancy letters proclaiming:

Tonkawa Sisters
Plumbing, Heating, and Air Conditioning

Rilla froze.

Sparrow had hired the Tonkawa sisters to install central air conditioning throughout Harmony House before summer's heat made the B & B as unbearable as it had been last summer—especially the attic.

Today the sisters were scheduled to install a ceiling fan in Rilla's room to further cool it down on hot summer nights.

Rilla had been eagerly awaiting their arrival. But that was yesterday—before two monsters came to life in her attic.

Dropping her bike, she took off like someone whose knees didn't hurt. Racing upstairs, her mind began to whirl.

How could she perform a monster disappearing act before the Tonkawa sisters climbed those forty-seven steps to her attic?

9
THE TONKAWA SISTERS

Fumbling with the lock, Rilla burst into the attic, dumping the bag of monster groceries in the middle of the floor.

Chelsea she wasn't worried about. All Rilla had to do was shut the bathroom door and hope the mermaid didn't splash too loudly.

Burly was another story.

There he was. Napping under a rabbit and a fox (both stuffed). On the radio, monotone voices discussing "fashion in women's tennis" must have lulled him to sleep.

Rilla clicked off the radio and poked him. "Hey. Wake up."

Poking a sleeping monster did *not* endear you to him.

Burly shoved her hand away and rolled over, snuggling between a giraffe and a camel. Should she leave him be? Would the Tonkawa sisters notice if one of the stuffed animals was snoring?

Too risky.

Rilla heard voices coming down the blue hallway.

Thinking fast, she scooped Burly into her arms and lifted him from his cozy spot. Kneeling, she scooted him under the bed.

He grumble-snored, but stayed put.

"Hel-lo-o?" came a voice as someone tapped on the door.

"*Please* stay here," Rilla implored him. "And be quiet."

In came the Tonkawa sisters, one carrying a ladder and one carrying the ceiling fan.

They were identical twins, with cropped hair (dyed orangy-red), matching tool belts, orange overalls, and orange caps sporting the logo

> *Hot or Cold, Wet or Dry,*
> *We're Your Gals; Give Us a Try*

"Hi," said Rilla.

"Hi," the sisters answered in unison.

"I'm Dottie," one said. "This is my sister, Lottie."

"Let's see where we're gonna put this thang," grumbled Lottie, frowning at the ceiling. "We'll have to move the bed."

"No!"

The sisters gaped at Rilla. "It's all right, love," Dottie said. "We'll move it back when we're finished."

"But it's a *water* bed. It weighs a zillion tons; you can't move it."

"Figures." Lottie scowled at the bed. "Let's go find the breaker box and start running wires." She dumped the fan onto the floor.

Dottie patted her twin on the arm. "Now, sis, we don't *have* to move the bed. I'll fetch another ladder."

Lottie grunted. "We'll be back, kid. If-it's-o-kay-with-you."

Boy, was she sarcastic.

Dottie smiled apologetically as the sisters left.

Rilla slumped against the wall. "That was close," she whispered.

Grabbing the grocery bag, she burrowed into her closet, shoving shoes aside to sprinkle golf tees and Cracker Jacks on the floor. Next she tore up two baseball cards.

Something stumbled over her legs. Burly. The scent of monster food must have tiptoed into his dream and woken him. He pushed her out of his way and reached for a handful of golf tees.

"Okay, I'm leaving," she told him. "Eat quietly."

Rilla backed out of the closet on hands and knees. "I have to shut the door," she added, "but I'll let you out as soon as the coast is clear."

Rilla peeked into the bathroom. Chelsea seemed fine,

although wide awake. She'd snitched a shampoo bottle, a sponge, and a long-handled brush off the shelf and was playing with them.

"I'll feed you after the Tonkawa sisters leave," Rilla promised.

Chelsea slapped the water with the back of the brush, meaning, Rilla assumed, the delay wasn't acceptable.

The sisters returned.

They planted ladders on each side of the bed and created a walkway with a thick board. Dottie covered Rilla's quilt with a sheet of plastic while Lottie positioned herself in the middle of the board and turned on a hand drill. The noise was loud enough to wake Rilla's entire collection of stuffed animals. Wouldn't *that* be a hoot?

Shutting off the drill, Lottie blew away plaster dust. "You don't have to stay and supervise." She wrinkled her nose at Rilla the same way she'd wrinkled it at the hole in the ceiling.

"I'm not supervising you. I have homework to do." Rilla stepped over Dottie's power cord and settled in at the desk.

Lottie raised a suspicious eyebrow. "How could you have homework? Isn't school out for the summer?"

"I'm home-schooled," Rilla explained. "This is my summer project."

Lottie scoffed, but Dottie seemed impressed.

Rilla dumped papers from her math notebook into

the trash. No need to save them anymore. She added fresh sheets and changed the label on the spine from *Math* to *Summer Project*.

Then she opened to page one.

So. How did authors begin a book? By making up a title?

Leaning back to think, Rilla tried not to look at Lottie, for fear she'd be accused again of supervising.

At the top of page one Rilla wrote: *Earth's Herbal Cures.* As an afterthought she added: *and Home Remedies,* since Sparrow said she could.

Step two. The author's byline? Beneath the title she scribbled: *by Rilla Harmony Earth.*

What came next? A dedication? She couldn't dedicate the book to Joshua Banks because her mother would see it. Maybe she should dedicate it to her father because it would bug Sparrow. And it *might* bug Sparrow enough to bring up the dreaded topic with her daughter. *Mmm.*

This book is dedicated to my father, David Charles Pinowski.

Next came the table of contents:

Chapter One—Cuts and Scrapes.

Chapter Two—?

How many chapters did it take to make a whole book?

Rilla sighed. Writing a book was hard work.

A loud burp exploded in the attic.

Burly! He'd gobbled his lunch too fast.

An appalled Lottie glowered at Rilla.

"Excuse me." Rilla ducked her head in embarrassment. *Please hurry and finish and get out of my attic,* she pleaded silently.

"Is this a bathroom?" Dottie asked, tapping a drill bit against the door.

"Yes, but you'll have to use the guest bath downstairs," Rilla told her. "The, uh, toilet is broken." She groaned. Monsters had turned her into a fibber.

The sisters laughed.

Rilla hadn't meant to be funny.

Dottie hoisted the fan up to her twin. "I'm a plumber, love. If your toilet is broken, I can fix it. And I don't need to *use* the bathroom; I just wondered about the music. Is it a radio?"

"Radio?" Rilla stopped to listen. Faint mermaid music floated under the door and swirled enticingly around the attic. "Oh, *that.*"

She wished Chelsea's songs weren't so appealing and exotic. "Um, it's a favorite tape of mine."

"Oh, it's a tape," Dottie said. "Quite lovely."

Lottie sniffed. "Sounds like New Age crap to me."

Rilla's stomach began to hurt. Covering up for monster noises was too difficult. She closed her eyes. *Let them believe whatever they want—as long as they don't ask the name of the tape.*

"What's the name of the tape, love?" Dottie asked.

Rilla's stomach lurched. How could she make Chelsea shut up?

"Um, it's called *An Evening Under the Sea*," she fudged. *Please don't ask who recorded it.*

"Who recorded it?"

Rilla wished she could dash for the Pepto-Bismol, but she could not open the bathroom door.

Putting both hands into her lap, she crossed her fingers. "It's a group called Chelsea and the Mermaids. Nobody's ever heard of them."

At least the last part was true.

Lottie aimed a screwdriver at her twin. "Leave the kid alone. She's doing homework."

Rilla turned back to the table of contents and wrote *Stomachaches* after *Chapter Two.*

Ka-thunka-thunka-thunka.

Oh, no.

Sudden thumpings from the closet threatened to drown out the mermaid music.

Please don't ask about the ka-thunkas.

Rilla knew they'd never believe her if she said it was another group called Burly and the Ballplayers. Ugh.

She hunched over her summer project notebook. The only good part about the Tonkawas invading her attic was that it forced her to start writing the book. "I can list afflictions," she mumbled to a blank page, "but I can't fill in the remedies until I look them up in Sparrow's herb books."

Lottie was glaring at her again.

"Sorry," Rilla said. "I'm talking to myself."

"Well, *I'm* talking to *you*, kid. We're finished. Come here and let me show you how this thingamajig works."

Rilla moved closer for the demonstration. Lottie showed her how to increase the fan speed and pull the chain to change the direction of the blades.

Meanwhile Dottie shook out the plastic sheet and folded it. She took down the ladders and gathered up tools.

Rilla swept pieces of clipped wires and plaster dust into a pile so Lottie could zap them with the cordless Mini-Vac she wore on her tool belt.

After Rilla assured Dottie that the attic toilet wasn't broken enough to warrant fixing *and* that the New Age bookstore downtown probably carried tapes similar to ones by the mermaid singers, the sisters packed up their equipment and clunked down the stairs.

Even though it was time for dinner, Rilla locked the door and collapsed onto the bed, holding her head in both hands.

Her stomachache had turned into a headache, which meant she now had a topic for chapter three.

Was this the headache Mother Lazuli had predicted? Or had Mother L.'s "powers" *caused* the headache?

Either way, the pain had arrived right on schedule, just like she said it would. And not even a double dose of Sparrow's feverfew could stop the miserable throbbing.

10
UGLY HAIR DAY

A shaft of sunlight poked Rilla in the eye, waking her.

Disoriented, she sat up, squinting at numbers on the clock. Half-past nine—in the morning!

Wow, Sparrow's herbal tea concoction really worked.

Rilla yawned. Her headache was gone, and so were the aches and pains from her bike accident. She felt terrific. All of yesterday's worries had melted away with the soreness.

The school year was over. She'd survived.

Rilla lay back down. Summer stretched out before her like a daisy-bordered road, leading to one pleasant adventure after another.

A distant sound of running bathwater met her ears.

Chelsea!

Rilla sprang from bed, but before she could make it to the bathroom, another noise drew her attention.

Burly was perched on the dresser, twirling the dial on the radio.

Rilla quickly twirled it back to the sports station. A voice was discussing the pros and cons of a summer football league.

The monster sprawled on his tummy to listen.

Rilla padded across the room and clicked on the new ceiling fan, marveling at the Tonkawa sisters' work. As she stepped into the bathroom, an angry mermonster greeted her by flopping about in a full-to-capacity tub. Water cascaded over the sides with every tail splash.

"What are you doing?" Rilla twisted the faucets, shutting off the water.

Chelsea dove under, searching the bottom of the tub.

She's looking for food because you fell asleep last night without feeding her.

Oh. Rilla filled a tumbler with water from the sink and poured in a generous amount of sea salt. Twisting open three kelp capsules, she sprinkled the light brown contents into the water, stirring it with one finger. "Here," she said, thrusting the glass at Chelsea.

The mermaid surfaced. She shook her wild hair, spraying water across the room, drenching Rilla and the already wet floor. Snatching the glass, Chelsea paused, pouting.

"I'll bring you tuna later," Rilla promised. "I can't keep an open can in the attic; the tuna would spoil. Then

I'd have a sick mermaid on my hands—and a smelly bedroom."

Chelsea listened, but didn't look pleased.

Rilla mopped up the floor with the bath mat, stopping at the mirror. Her reflection made her flinch.

She still wore yesterday's shirt—now rumpled—and ripped shorts. Her fancy hairdo looked as tangly as Chelsea's. Might take all summer to unravel the beads and braids. Better get started.

Clank, clank, clank!

That was Sparrow, banging a spoon on the water pipes, which ran straight from the kitchen to the attic. It meant, *Get downstairs. Pronto.*

Sparrow clanked the pipes a lot on cold winter mornings when Rilla slept in because the attic was dark and freezing. But why was she clanking today? The first morning of summer vacation?

"Wait till I unravel my hair," Rilla grumbled, resting her elbows on a shelf to keep her arms from getting tired.

CLANK, CLANK, CLANK!

"Rats."

She'd better make herself presentable *fast* and go see what her mother wanted. Living in a house full of strangers meant she couldn't jump out of bed and run downstairs in pajamas, tousled hair, and a sleep-wrinkled face.

Smoothing her clothes the best she could, Rilla splashed her cheeks with cold water. Lifting her cowboy hat from the top of the bedpost, she stuffed her hair beneath the hat to hide it.

Sparrow greeted her at the bottom of the steps. "How do you feel?"

"Fine." Rilla nodded at Mother Lazuli, who sat on a stool at the counter, sipping tea. (Probably Queen of the Meadow, the tea she drank to dissolve her gallstones.)

Today's tent dress was azure, with matching earrings, bracelets, and necklaces in various hues of her trademark color.

"We didn't wake you for dinner last night," Sparrow explained. "We thought it best to let you sleep."

We? Rilla hated having *two* mothers whenever Lazuli showed up. "How'd you know I was sleeping?"

Sparrow looked at her as though she'd asked, *How do you know I'm your daughter?*

"Oh, right," Rilla muttered. Their resident seer could detect a sleeping teenager three flights up.

Sparrow bustled about the kitchen, placing items on a breakfast tray. "Sorry you missed Mother's dinner last night. She baked her wonderful goat-cheese bean loaf. I saved some for your lunch."

Whoopee! Rilla cheered silently. *Goat-cheese bean loaf. To die for.*

"Meanwhile," Sparrow continued, "I desperately need your help. Poppy is . . . well, under the weather today. You'll have to take over for her."

"Take over? You mean clean rooms? Do laundry? Change sheets?"

Sparrow peered over her glasses. "You got a problem with that?"

Rilla didn't mention the fact that it *was* her first day of vacation. "What's wrong with Aunt Poppy? Is she sick?"

Sparrow guffawed. "Let's just say she overpumped yesterday. She can't get out of bed because it involves moving muscles, and she doesn't have one left that isn't sore."

"Oh." Rilla couldn't hide her amusement as the two kitchen mothers exchanged exasperated glances.

"Take this breakfast tray to her," Sparrow ordered. "Then get back here fast and eat. By then I'll have a list of rooms ready to clean."

"Can't I take a shower first?"

Sparrow slammed a homemade napkin onto Aunt Poppy's tray. "There isn't time. Besides, you're bound to get dirtier. Take a shower after you've finished."

Rilla didn't want to spend the day wearing a cowboy hat and grungy clothes, but she didn't want Sparrow to ground her for the summer, either.

Picking up the tray, she hurried to the blue floor, knocking at the only door without a brass suite number.

"Come in," quivered a feeble voice.

The scent of incense almost knocked Rilla over as she stepped into the darkened room. Pausing, she let her eyes adjust to the dim light.

"Aunt Poppy? It's me! Your favorite niece! With breakfast!"

In the dark, somebody moaned.

Her aunt obviously didn't have a sense of humor today.

A lamp clicked on. Aunt Poppy, with hair in her eyes, blinked in bewilderment the way the monsters did whenever Rilla woke them.

While her aunt struggled to sit up without moving any muscles, Rilla's gaze traveled the room. Aunt Poppy loved needlepoint wall hangings. Like the one above the bed:

Eat, Drink, and Re-Marry

Rilla set the breakfast tray on Aunt Poppy's bedside table. "Have a nice day," she chirped.

"Yeah, right," her aunt mumbled.

On the way out, Rilla stopped to squint at Aunt Poppy's wedding pictures. All four of them. With different grooms. Her aunt's name used to be Sally Knox Bailey Hailey Hobbs Street. Now it was simply Poppy Harmony Earth.

Returning to the kitchen, Rilla realized how hungry she was after not eating dinner last night. She wolfed down a bowl of steaming couscous with grapes and pecans—something Sparrow called grape nut cereal, but it was nothing like the store-bought kind.

Rilla ate fast, listening to Mother Lazuli brag about

her daughter, Plum, who attended some far out boarding school in Sri Lanka called the One World School of Inner Consciousness (OWSIC).

"Get a move on," Sparrow urged. "We're booked full for Memorial Day weekend, and we don't want guests arriving before their rooms are ready."

Sparrow flipped a piece of paper onto the table in front of her. "Clean rooms in this order. Skip any with a Do Not Disturb sign. And hustle."

Rilla finished her cereal, anticipating a boring day.

It could be worse, her mind told her. *Mother Lazuli could have brought Plum along with her.*

Eww. Just thinking about the girl made Rilla cringe.

Obnoxious was too kind a word to describe her. Every stitch of clothing she wore was deep purple (to match her name) and bore the OWSIC logo, as if she didn't want you to forget how weird she was.

Plus, she always tried to act as psychic as her mother—but Rilla suspected she was faking it.

Rilla glanced at Mother Lazuli. Did the *all-knowing* sneer on her face mean she could read Rilla's nasty thoughts about dear Plum?

Yikes.

Rilla's instincts told her to make a fast getaway.

And she did.

But not before whisking a fresh can of tuna off the pantry shelf.

11

AN UNFAIR UNIVERSE

Scrubbing toilets, stripping beds, and piling fresh-and-folded towels onto countless shelves was *not* the ideal way to spend a sunny Saturday.

Rilla's clothes became even grungier, and her muscles began to ache from running up and down stairs from the suites to the washer and dryer in the basement.

At noon, she took a break to check on the monsters.

Chelsea had snarfed down the tuna and was floating and sleeping at the same time.

A baseball game blared from the radio. Burly was in monster heaven on top of the dresser, bear ears glued to the commentary.

Satisfied, Rilla hurried outside to feed the kittens before Sparrow could bug her about it. Stepping into the barn, she relished the cooler air. "Oreo?" she called. "Here kitties."

Lifting a bag of cat crunchies off a shelf, she sprinkled them into two bowls, then filled another dish with water from a jug.

Cat sounds echoed from around the barn. The mama cat and one of her kittens darted from a dark corner, diving for the food.

The other two scampered in from outside, tumbling over each other to get to their bowls. It made Rilla feel guilty for not feeding them earlier.

"Sorry, guys," she muttered. "I'm having a bad day." She wondered if cats ever had bad days.

Milk Dud, Pepsi, and Dorito were seven months old now. Sparrow hadn't mentioned getting rid of them, and Rilla never brought it up. She loved the kittens. They were much easier to get along with than monsters (or mothers).

Besides, there would never be another litter. Mr. Tamerow had talked Sparrow into getting Oreo "fixed," even though Sparrow had argued about "fooling Mother Nature."

Mr. T. sent a chart showing how one cat and her kittens can contribute 420,000 offspring to the world in seven years. Sparrow finally relented and took Oreo to the vet.

Picking up feisty Dorito (her favorite), Rilla cuddled him, remembering the day she'd spitefully chosen names for the cats. It was an act of revenge after Sparrow made her refuse treats from the home-schoolers' Halloween party. (Like it would kill an Earth to eat a bag of candy.)

Dorito sprang from her arms. Rilla chased him

around Aunt Poppy's Backyard Ride-a-Mower until Sparrow called her to lunch.

Returning the water jug and food bag to the shelf, Rilla made sure the barn door was propped open wide enough for the cats to come and go.

Heading back to the house, Rilla moved slowly up the flagstone walkway, choosing the best rocks along the way. Might as well start collecting them to create an island home for Chelsea.

"Hi."

She straightened with a jerk.

It was Joshua Banks! Where had *he* come from?

Rilla's blood ran hot and cold at the same time.

He eyed her with curiosity. "What are you doing?"

Shock consumed her. Here she stood, wearing the same clothes he'd seen her in yesterday, only wrinkled and ripped, with her stupid cowboy hat yanked over her eyebrows, and two handfuls of rocks.

If that wasn't bad enough, both knees were graced with bandages, now dirty from kneeling to clean tile.

Please let me die. Right here. Halfway between the barn and the house. My life is over.

Joshua cocked his head, waiting for an answer.

Rilla debated an urge to drop the rocks, dash back to the barn, and hide behind the Ride-a-Mower.

Later she could tell him: "*Oh, that wasn't me. It was my weird cousin, Plum. We look alike, but she collects rocks and never changes her clothes or shows the world her hair or knees.*"

"Hi," she said instead. "I'm, um, collecting rocks for the aquarium."

He laughed. Was it funny?

"If you put in *that* many rocks, there won't be room for the fish."

"Oh, right." She dropped a few.

"What's with the bandages?" He motioned toward her knees.

Rilla glanced at them as if she didn't know they were there. "I sorta tried to fly, but crashed and burned."

He laughed again, which was okay since she was trying to be funny.

"So what are *you* doing?" she asked, hoping to redirect his attention.

"A few of us are getting up a softball game at Willow Park. Thought you'd make a good second base to my shortstop."

His grin almost ironed the wrinkles out of her shorts.

I'd make a good second base to his shortstop?

Rilla hesitated. One, because Sparrow wouldn't let her leave until the B & B rooms were finished, and two, even if she *could* go, she wouldn't. Not without a major makeover. "I can't."

Did his pout mean he was disappointed that she, Rilla Harmony Earth, couldn't go? Or because he needed one more body to make two teams?

"My aunt is . . . sick," she told him, forgoing an explanation. "I have to help around the B & B today—which is why I'm dressed like this." *Yes! Now he understands why I look so awful.*

"Well, okay." He jogged toward the alley. "I'll stop by some other time."

Some other time? her mind echoed as she watched him leave. *When?*

"Your bean loaf is getting cold!" Sparrow hollered out the back door.

Rilla cringed, immensely grateful Joshua Banks was out of earshot before the bean loaf announcement was bellowed across the backyard.

Shoving the smallest rocks into her pockets, she stormed toward the house, angry at the unfairness of a universe that would allow her one true love to witness her in such disarray.

According to the "Legend of the Global Monsters," good fortune was destined to come her way from "spotting a mini-monster in the wild."

Well, where *was* her good fortune?

Thankyouverymuch.

She kicked a rock, angry at the universe—and at Sparrow.

And at Mother Lazuli and her stupid goat-cheese bean loaf.

12
MONSTER BALL

It was ten A.M., and Sparrow hadn't clanked on the pipes yet.

Maybe Aunt Poppy was back in business. She *had* to act normal today because José was coming to play at a Memorial Day concert in town.

Rilla suspected her aunt was sweet on José. If not, why did she always spruce up whenever he was around? Last visit, her ripped-jeans-and-T-shirt cleaning clothes gave way to a silk blouse and skirt.

Good thing José had booked a room at Harmony House a year ago, or he'd be out of luck. The B & B was overflowing this holiday weekend. Rilla'd never seen so many guests lounging in the parlor to read, watch TV, or sip iced mango tea—available twenty-four hours a day.

Sparrow had banished the weight machine to the

barn. Assisted by several guests, Aunt Poppy had set it up next to her Ride-a-Mower.

Sparrow had even banished Mother Lazuli—ha! She'd had to relinquish her suite on the blue floor and move into Rilla's classroom to sleep on Sparrow's ancient futon with the peace symbol pattern.

Rilla forced herself to stop daydreaming and concentrate on what she was doing. Writing in her journal. The one Sparrow and Aunt Poppy had snitched in her dream the night the monsters came to life.

It wasn't really a journal, but a small notebook filled with . . . well, information and observations about . . . well, Joshua Banks, to be exact.

Stashed inside the notebook's spiral binder was a pencil he'd once lent her, complete with his teeth marks on it. Folded between pages one and two were his school papers she'd rescued from the Earths' trash can.

This morning, the first line of a poem kept wiggling into her brain. She wanted to jot it down before it wiggled out again:

It's summer, and my one true love . . .

That was it. What came next? A line that rhymed with *love*?

Dove. Glove. Above. Shove.

Out of the zillions of love songs on the radio, Rilla couldn't believe there were so few words that rhymed with *love*.

She thought up a lot of stupid lines. (Like: *sent from*

heaven up above.) And *really* stupid lines. (Like: *asked me if I'd wear his glove.*)

Thinking up a line that made sense was impossible.

Oh, well, she'd leave the snippet, along with other half poems she'd started about her one true love. (Nothing rhymed with Joshua, either.)

Time to get dressed. Rilla stashed the journal back inside her cookie tin and headed for the bathroom.

Taking extra care this morning, she showered and shampooed, then picked out her favorite summer shorts outfit (red plaid) to balance out how horrible she'd looked yesterday. She even put on lip gloss, taped fresh bandages on both knees, and combed bangs over the new scab on her forehead.

Rilla smiled into the tiny bathroom mirror. She looked good—except for her wet, stringy hair. Should she braid it again?

While contemplating the hour she'd spent untangling the braids and how awful they'd looked, Chelsea emerged from the water and perched on the edge of the tub.

Smiling at the mermaid, Rilla admired her Aruba simulation.

It had taken hours last night to smuggle everything to the attic without Sparrow and Mother Lazuli becoming suspicious. But it was worth it.

Rocks and ferns from the backyard covered the bottom of the tub, giving Chelsea a few keen hiding places.

Okay, so it didn't *look* like the Caribbean, but it *did* look more "oceany."

Before bed, Rilla had even serenaded her monster children on the ukulele Mr. Tamerow had sent from Maui.

Chelsea began to jabber and point.

Rilla tried to translate what the mermaid wanted. She didn't stop jabbering until Rilla handed over the comb and the box of tiny beads.

"*You* want to braid my hair?" Astonished, Rilla knelt beside the tub, bunching the bath mat under her sore knees.

The mermaid whisked the comb through Rilla's hair, expertly dividing it into sections with pins.

Holding still was easy. Every time Rilla wiggled, Chelsea poked her with the comb.

The sea monster worked swiftly, singing a song about stormy seas and wind-bent palms. Rilla didn't know *how* she knew; the music just seemed to tell the story without people words.

Burly peeked around the door. Venturing closer, he watched and listened as he tossed his mini-basketball into the air and caught it.

Finally the mermaid gave her a little pat. Rilla stood and peered into the mirror. Five tiny braids hung from each side of her center part. Colorful beads were woven smartly into the hair, staggered at different lengths.

Rilla loved it. It looked incredibly nifty, like she'd just

returned from the islands. She started to hug Chelsea, but the mermaid slipped into the water, dipping under to skim between the rocks and greenery.

Just as well. Hugging a wet monster didn't seem very pleasant.

Rilla returned to her desk. Before going down to breakfast, she wanted to jot a few more ideas for her summer project.

Last night—in between trips for tub rocks—she'd lugged Sparrow's herb books to the attic. Every reference to cuts and scrapes mentioned tea tree oil, so her mother had been right on target.

Other remedies for cuts included aloe vera, marigold, bistort, comfrey, and white oak bark. Rilla recognized some of the herbs, but others—like bistort—called for more research. This wasn't going to be easy.

Under stomachache remedies, she found all the things Sparrow gave her in lieu of the pink drink: ginger, peppermint, blue vervain, wild yam, marshmallow, and comfrey (again).

Thump!

Burly's basketball bounced across Rilla's desk and hit her in the chin. Catching it, she lofted it back to the monster. Was he jealous that she'd spent so much time with Chelsea this morning?

If so, she'd feed him first. Setting aside her book, she sprinkled golf tees, Cracker Jacks, and a Don Mattingly baseball card on her desk.

Keeping the monsters stocked with food would slowly drain her life's savings. She hoped Soozi's Sporting Goods soon had another sale.

Opening a fresh can of tuna from her stash in the dresser, Rilla dumped it onto a paper plate, sprinkled kelp on top, then headed into the bathroom to feed Chelsea.

Splash!

That was the basketball landing in the tub.

"Bur-ly!" The splash drenched Rilla's shirt. She blotted herself with a towel, then fished for the ball.

Chelsea snatched it from her grasp and took a dive.

Burly's eyebrows shot to heaven. He began to grumble-growl.

Chelsea hid the ball under greenery. Sitting on top of it, she giggled at Burly. Bubbles of mirth rose to the surface and popped in the air.

The sports monster scrambled up the towel hamper.

Rilla lunged to keep him from diving headfirst into the tub. "Give back the ball!" she shouted, wondering if the mermaid could hear underwater.

Burly struggled against her, but she kept a tight grip while removing the plate of tuna and kelp she'd just set on the shelf.

When the mermaid saw her food disappear, she shot to the surface to protest. The ball bobbed up beside her.

Rilla scooped it from the water before Chelsea could react.

Hurrying out, she dumped Burly and the wet ball onto the floor and shut the bathroom door. "Better keep you two apart. No more monster ball."

An instant later, the basketball came barreling toward her face. Rilla blocked it with both arms, letting it bounce to the floor.

Burly guffawed (more or less) at her clumsy miss.

"Okay, I'll play with you," Rilla told him, hoping she'd wear him out soon so he'd crawl onto her pillow for a nap.

Tap, tap, tap.

Rilla froze. No one *ever* knocked on her door.

Except the Tonkawa sisters, her brain reminded her.

She glanced at the ceiling fan. It was fine. No need for a return service call from Dottie and her evil twin.

"Who is it?" she called, her voice a nervous whimper.

TAP, TAP, TAP.

Rilla whirled, rolling the basketball beneath the bed.

Burly dove after it. Mercifully out of sight.

Quickly she opened the door—one inch.

And caught her breath.

Standing on the top step was her one true love.

Stunned, Rilla leaped back.

The door swung open, and Joshua Banks popped in.

Joshua Banks! In her attic!

Flomp!

The damp basketball hit Joshua squarely in the stomach with such force, it crumpled him against the closet door.

TWEEEEET! TWEEEEET!

That was a double blast from Burly's whistle.

"What—?!" Joshua huffed, gasping for breath.

Then his jaw fell open as he gaped at the sight before him: A monster, wearing short pants and a rugby shirt, jumped up and down on the water bed, pointing a scrappy paw at him and chitter-laughing at his awkward fumble.

13

AN OFFER YOU CAN'T REFUSE

A stunned Joshua Banks clutched the basketball to his stomach, but his eyes never left the spectacle on Rilla's bed.

Rilla was paralyzed. She couldn't move; she couldn't speak. She simply gaped at Joshua while *he* gaped at Burly.

The thought that *should* have been frantically racing through her mind was: *My monster secret is out! How will I explain it to Joshua?*

But that's *not* what was racing through her mind at all. Lighting up her brain like a billboard was:

> Joshua, My Joshua, Is Standing Here
> in My Very Own Attic—
> and This Time—I Look Terrific!

Everything in Rilla's world should have been absolutely perfect at this one frozen moment in time—or *would* have been perfect—if only Joshua Banks was gazing at *her* the way he was gazing at Burly.

"That is so cool," Joshua finally stammered, inching toward the bed. "It actually threw the ball to me. Where'd you get it?"

"Huh?"

"I mean, did you get it for your birthday? Or Christmas?"

Rilla closed the door, just to be safe.

She couldn't concentrate on Joshua's naive questions when the biggest question of all was stampeding through her brain like a herd of endangered rhinos—WHY IS JOSHUA BANKS HERE?

He circled the bed.

Burly pivoted, locked in a staring match with Joshua.

Or was the monster merely waiting to catch the ball?

Rilla cleared her throat. "Um, what are you, um, doing here?"

"Oh." Joshua finally looked at her.

Then he did a double take, as if noticing she looked pretty darn good—or at least better than she'd looked yesterday.

The double take pleased her as much as his surprise visit was flabbergasting her.

"Well," Joshua began. "I came by to see if you

wanted to go to a movie with us this afternoon. I called first, but your line's been busy forever."

One disadvantage of living in a B & B during the busy season.

"Your mom told me to come on up." He glanced around. "Cool room."

Rilla shifted positions, pleased to know her arms and legs still worked. "I, um, guess I owe you an explanation," she said. "About him."

She gestured toward Burly, who now acted frustrated because Joshua was hanging on to the ball. He began to chide the boy in monster talk as he tried to snatch it out of Joshua's hands.

Laughing, Joshua teased him, offering the ball, then yanking it away. "How do you turn him on and off?"

"Excuse me?"

Dropping the ball, Joshua began to poke at Burly's stomach. "Is there a switch? Or do you wind him up? How many batteries does he take?"

Burly grabbed the ball and tried to scoot away, but Joshua swooped him off the bed to search for wires and a hidden battery compartment.

"He feels so real," Joshua exclaimed.

Rilla began to laugh.

The trauma of the last five minutes cascaded so many emotions through her, the only way she could react was to give in to the ridiculousness of it all.

"Are you okay?" Joshua let go of the monster and peered at Rilla.

She could not stop laughing. *He thinks Burly runs on batteries!*

"What's wrong?" Joshua shoved his fingertips into his jean pockets, looking flustered. "What did I do?"

Rilla gasped for breath, hoping her face wasn't all red and splotchy.

"You didn't do anything. We just need to, um, talk." She pointed toward the Navajo braided rug on the floor. "Sit. This may take a while."

Joshua, a bewildered look on his face, sprawled on the rug.

Burly hurled the ball at him.

This time, Joshua caught it.

The monster chitter-cheered as Joshua gave him a thumbs-up sign.

Rilla chuckled at how fast boy and monster were bonding. She knelt on the rug. "I know you're not going to believe me," she began, "but—"

Burly was making so much noise, Rilla had to raise her voice.

Then Chelsea launched into a shrill lullaby, adding to the commotion.

"Why don't you shut him off so we can talk?" Joshua asked, glancing around the attic, searching for the source of the other noises.

"What I'm trying to tell you is . . ." Rilla paused,

winding one of her mini-braids through her fingers as she searched for words of explanation. "I *can't* shut him off."

Starting at the beginning, she told Joshua about the anonymous gift card that arrived last Christmas from the Monster of the Month Club headquarters in Oklahoma City. (She left out the part about wondering if the card had come from him.)

She told him of the arrival of Icicle, the January Selection, and how shocked she'd been to receive a real, live monster.

Joshua's cheek began to twitch.

He doesn't believe you.

Sighing, Rilla had no choice but to continue. She told him about the February monster, Sweetie Pie, and how she'd managed to keep the two a secret from her mother and aunt. And how Shamrock had shown up stuffed and silent, the way the monsters were *supposed* to arrive.

Rilla plucked the three monsters from her bed and showed them to Joshua, telling him how she learned Mr. Tamerow was the giver of the gift.

Then she burrowed into her cookie tin to retrieve the "Legend of the Global Monsters" and read it to him, telling how the stars had shifted, breaking the magic. How the monsters had continued to come, month after month. Then how the magic was sparked again—last Friday morning—bringing the April and May monsters to life.

Joshua touched Icicle gingerly, as if expecting him to spring to his paws. "April *and* May?" he echoed. "You mean, there's another one?"

"Yes." She watched his face, realizing how bizarre the whole story sounded. *Please don't think I'm weird like Tina says,* her mind pleaded.

Burly had given up on his new playmate. Burrowing into the stuffed animals on Rilla's pillow, he curled into a monster ball for nap time.

Joshua cocked his head. "You know, Earth, this is *real* hard to believe."

"I had trouble believing it myself." She nodded toward the bathroom. "Open the door and meet the April monster."

"No kidding?" Joshua's eyes nearly tripled in size. Rilla followed him into the bathroom.

Chelsea perched on the edge of the tub, tail dangling in the water. She was braiding her hair, weaving shiny beads into each green braid.

"Hey!" Rilla exclaimed. "You snitched my beads."

Chelsea gave her a smug look.

"It's a mermaid!" Joshua whisper-gasped.

"I know," Rilla replied, as if everyone harbored a mermaid in their bathtub. "Her name is Chelsea and she's from Aruba."

Rilla forgave the mermaid for stealing the beads because they looked so stunning in her hair, along with the shells and tiny starfish.

"Wow." Joshua tiptoed closer to peer at her.

The mermaid flung a bronze bead at him. It hit him on the nose and bounced into the tub.

"Chel-sea!" Rilla was mortified.

Joshua backed away, rubbing his nose. "What's the other monster's name?" he asked, jabbing a thumb toward the bedroom.

"Burly. From Argentina. Come on, I'll show you their, um, *birth announcements.*"

Rilla took the monthly selection cards from her cookie tin, making sure Joshua didn't see the journal with his name in it.

He read the monster cards, adding a "Wow" after each one. "This is the most amazing thing anyone has ever told me." He gaped at her in awe.

Rilla wished she, alone, was the one who awed him, yet she knew he was monster-awed. "Promise me you'll never tell a soul," she whispered.

Joshua looked disappointed. "But—"

"Promise," Rilla insisted, suddenly panicked at the thought of Joshua telling Andrew, Andrew telling Wally, Wally telling Marcia and Kelly and Tina. *Oh, gosh, not Tina.* "*Please* promise."

Joshua raised his right hand. "Okay, Earth, I promise." His cheek began to twitch again. "Under one condition."

"Condition?" Rilla's panic returned to flush her face and make her voice squeak. "*What* condition?"

Joshua grinned his double dimpled grin. "On the condition that you'll let me play ball with Burly—anytime I want."

Mmm. An offer you can't refuse . . .

Relieved, Rilla returned his grin. *This could be good,* she told herself. *This could be REAL good.*

"Fine," she said. "It's a deal."

And Rilla shook hands with her one true love.

14

A BELATED PREDICTION

The kitchen was much too crowded.

Sparrow and Mother Lazuli were at the counter, poring over old cookbooks, discussing ways to revamp favorite recipes into healthier fare. (Like substituting cheese with tofu.) Rilla thought it sounded like a sure way to *ruin* favorite recipes.

Long-haired José had arrived, guitar case in hand, a backpack slung over one shoulder. He always traveled light to his "gigs," as he called them.

Aunt Poppy was fussing over him while fixing a plate of fruit salad topped with yogurt and pumpkin seeds, with carrot bran muffins on the side.

"Hey," said José when he noticed Rilla. He moved the Sunday paper from a chair so she could sit next to him and bring him up to date on her life. (A censored version, with no mention of monsters or her one true love.)

After she finished, Rilla delved into the newspaper while José returned his attention to Aunt Poppy and brunch. In spite of all the distractions, only one thought consumed her this morning: She was going to a movie with Joshua Banks. (Well, okay, with the *other* home-schoolers too.)

Still, Joshua had personally come to her house to invite her. (Well, okay, her phone was busy. . . .)

Rilla peeked over the top of the newspaper to observe her aunt. Maybe she could pick up a few tips on how to flirt with the opposite sex:

1. Laugh at everything he says.
2. Touch his arm when you speak to him.
3. Maintain heavy eye contact.
4. Move like the Tin Man in *The Wizard of Oz* before Dorothy oiled his joints.

Ha. Cancel number four. Rilla knew her aunt was really trying to act normal despite her sore muscles. José was too polite to inquire about her awkward movements.

Sparrow and Mother Lazuli joined everyone at the table. Mother L. immediately launched a discussion about her favorite topic: daughter Plum.

Plum was a year older than Rilla and already working toward a degree in naturopathy—which aggravated Rilla since she didn't know what the word meant and had to look it up in the dictionary. (Healing by means of natural methods: sunshine, air, water, and herbs—meaning Plum would become yet another herb freak.)

Concentrating on the Sunday paper was impossible with everyone yapping. Rilla skipped to the comics while finishing her plate of fruit. Besides, she found the pre-Father's Day sale ads too annoying. Anything that reminded of her father these days annoyed her.

Rilla glanced at José. What if Aunt Poppy married him? What if they filled the B & B with children? Then Harmony House would have a resident father. (Rilla had never imagined a father with long hair and an earring, but José was nice and had taught her how to play her ukulele.)

She tried to picture Aunt Poppy as a mother. Mmm. After four tries at marriage, would she want children on try number five?

The clock chimed noon. Rilla quickly folded the newspaper and cleaned up her dishes. She needed at least a half hour to feed the kittens, check on the monsters, and decide what to wear to the movie.

"Where are you off to?" Sparrow asked.

"The movies."

"Alone?"

"No, um, with Joshua Banks and—"

"Ewww," teased Aunt Poppy. "Ril-la has a da-ate."

Rilla felt her face turn as red as the organically grown

strawberries she'd just eaten. "It's not a date. The others are going too."

This triggered a discussion of "first dates." Everyone began to relate personal stories, giving Rilla a chance to slip away without more ribbing.

In the attic, Rilla found Burly in the bathroom, playing catch with Chelsea, who was actually returning the ball this time.

"Good job, Bur," Rilla exclaimed. "You taught her how to play *nicely.*"

He seemed frustrated since his partner's playing field was limited to the length and width of the tub. Still, he acted pleased by Rilla's compliment.

Stopping the game, he followed her into the closet.

"I'm not coming in here to feed you," she told him.

He stayed anyway, watching with curiosity as she sorted through her skimpy summer wardrobe.

Rilla had been cool about this whole movie thing until Aunt Poppy had called it a *date.* Now she felt panicky. *Was* this her first date? With her one true love? Could it *be* a first date if the others were there?

Standing in front of the mirror, Rilla tried on each outfit. Burly sat on top of her desk to watch and chatter his approval or disapproval:

Pink dress—no.

Tie-dyed T-shirt—no.

Shorts set with the matching vest—no.

The red plaid outfit she'd started out with—no.

"What, then?" she asked him.

Burly burrowed through her closet again—and her dresser, then handed her a long tee with a colorful geometric design. The design perfectly matched the mauve leggings Burly had found in her pajama drawer, *plus* blended well with the beads in her braids.

Mmm. Rilla put on the ensemble and stepped into her clogs. She looked terrific—completely color coordinated. Mrs. Welter would be proud.

Burly tilted his head, giving her an approving once over.

How did a sports monster from Argentina develop such a sense for summer fashion? "Thank you," she told him. "*Sassy* magazine should hire you and Chelsea as hair and fashion consultants."

Shrugging, Burly grabbed a baseball and headed back to Aruba.

Rilla made sure she had money and the monsters had plenty of food. "Be good," she told them. "And behave."

The blue hallway was filled with guests coming and going. Lots of new people had discovered Harmony House since Sparrow and Aunt Poppy had stepped up advertising.

Rilla didn't recognize any of the guests—except one. The one wearing blue and ambling down the hallway, squinting suspiciously at each door.

What was Mother Lazuli doing? Searching for monsters? *Yikes.*

Rilla whizzed past without stopping. Thank heavens the attic door was locked. . . .

As Rilla started down the curved stairway to the main floor, something familiar caught her eye: a Siberian herdsman hat with luggage keys dangling from one side.

"Mr. Tamerow!" Rilla shrieked, flying the rest of the way downstairs.

"Surprise!" He waved from the registration desk. "My travels have brought me to the friendliest B & B on earth—er, I mean, *with* the Earths."

Sparrow glanced up from the registration ledger to boo at his joke.

"Rilly, it's good to see you." Mr. Tamerow lifted her off the ground, swinging her around in a hug like he used to do when she was very young.

She returned his hug, embarrassed that he still treated her like a little girl. "I'm so glad you're here," she gushed. No matter what traumas were going on in her life, things always got better after Mr. Tamerow arrived.

"I have bad news," Sparrow said.

"What?" they asked in unison.

"There's no room in the inn." She looked apologetic.

"Oh," Mr. Tamerow replied. "Well, no problem. I'll camp out in Rilly's classroom; I've done it before."

"Sorry, Abe. Even the classroom is occupied."

Rilla glared at her mother. Was she really going to turn him away?

"Mother Lazuli is here," Sparrow explained.

"Ahhhh," he sighed, giving Rilla a *knowing look*. He was as big a fan of the self-proclaimed psychic as Rilla was.

She couldn't help but snicker.

"By the way," Sparrow added. "Mother knew you were coming. Well, not you in particular, but an *old family friend*. Since she knew we had a full house, she didn't mention it, so, unfortunately, I booked the last room only minutes ago."

"What good are her predictions if they come too late?" Rilla snipped.

One look from Sparrow hushed her.

"Not to worry." Mr. Tamerow lifted his well-worn traveling bag, splashed with stickers from every country Rilla had heard of and a few she hadn't. "I'll find a hotel," he said. "Call me a taxi."

"You're a taxi," Rilla teased.

Mr. Tamerow laughed as if he'd never heard the joke before, and she loved him for it.

Sparrow wasn't in the mood to laugh. "I'm really sorry, Abe."

Rilla stared at her mother. Surely she hadn't taken Mr. T.'s comment seriously. "That's it?" she blurted. "You're sending him away? To a hotel?"

"What do you want me to do? Put him up in the barn with the cats?"

Rilla considered the idea. Should she offer him the attic? How *could* she with monsters all about? And where would *she* sleep?

Mr. Tamerow patted her arm. "Don't get in a tizzy about it; I'll be fine. Tell you what." He snapped his fingers. "Let's all have dinner together. At some fancy restaurant. My treat."

It sounded wonderful. "Can we?" Rilla pleaded.

"I've got a better idea." Sparrow let the registration ledger fall shut. "Why don't you join us here for dinner? Mother is making her famous sushi lasagna with wasabi sauce and nori."

Mr. Tamerow hesitated.

"Oh, it's wonderful," Sparrow assured him. "Instead of pasta noodles, she layers the sauce with sheets of dried sea vegetables."

"My!" he exclaimed, as if it were a fabulous offer. "*That* certainly settles it." Turning sideways, he made a goofy face for Rilla's benefit. "I'll promptly check into a hotel and be back before dinnertime."

Rilla escorted him outside. "This is just awful," she said, sitting next to him on the veranda steps to wait for the taxi.

"Well, it's my fault for showing up unannounced," he told her. "Looks as though I need to make reservations like everyone else on the globe."

Rilla stared at his kind face and sparkly eyes. There were so many things she wanted to tell him—how two of the stuffed monsters had come to life again, how Joshua Banks had found out and wanted to *play* with one of them, how she was actually going to a movie with her one true love, and how Mother Lazuli had shown up and ruined her life.

But the only words that came out of her mouth were answers to his questions about the bandages on her knees and about her summer project. He even gave her a few personal afflictions to find remedies for: sore feet and aching muscles. Two problems plaguing world travelers.

A taxi pulled into the drive of the B & B.

Rilla squinted to see if it was the same driver she'd collided with.

It wasn't. Maybe the cabbie was already off to her wonderful new life in the lighthouse on the cape, as Mother Lazuli had predicted.

Mr. Tamerow rose and picked up his bags. "You know, Rilly, the worst tragedy of all is not that I can't stay at Harmony House."

"No?" *It's not spending time with me,* she added smugly to herself.

"No. The *worst* tragedy is that you and I have to face Mother Lazuli's sushi lasagna with wasabi sauce and nori."

Rilla laughed at his pained expression, then hugged him good-bye.

Wherever in the world her father was, Rilla hoped he was just like Mr. Tamerow. But then—if he was like Mr. T., he'd be here right now, with his very own daughter, staying forever at Harmony House.

Plus he'd be the kind of father who'd take her out on nights when Mother Lazuli cooked—for double cheeseburgers and double desserts!

15

EARTHS DON'T EAT SWEETS

In the dark movie theater, Rilla held her breath to squelch the sudden attack of hiccups that threatened to make her die of embarrassment.

Kelly kept giggling and poking her to stop. She was *trying* to stop.

Besides the hiccups, three other things bugged her:

1. The movie. *Mostly Midnight.* She'd already seen it—last weekend with Aunt Poppy—so she knew how it ended, *and* she knew there were five scary scenes, two good, the others not-so-good, plus two kissing scenes—both good. Real good.

2. The seating arrangement. (She'd been late, thanks to Mr. T.'s arrival.) The other home-schoolers were already seated. Girls in front; boys in back. Wally sat behind her and yanked on one of her braids every time something funny happened.

3. Tina Welter. *She* sat in back with the boys. With Joshua Banks, to be exact. Rilla was getting a kink in her neck trying to look at them without looking at them.

Why did Joshua invite me to the movie, then sit with Tina?

Hiccup.

She probably sat next to *him* instead of vice versa.

Hiccup, hiccup.

I should have stayed home and worked on my herb book.

The other home-schoolers' books had more interesting themes. Wally was writing *Inventing Fun-to-Eat Treats.* (A book bound to collect dust at Harmony House.) Andrew's book was *Animals of Australia.* (Where he was from.) Joshua's was *Sports in America.*

The girls' books were:

Marcia: *How to Invest Your Allowance.*

Kelly: *Making Your Own Movie.* (Sounded cool.)

Tina: *Dress to Impress.* (She probably devoted an entire chapter to matching socks to outfits.)

Rilla would have picked any of those topics over *herbs.*

At least coming to the movie had given her another malady for her book: hiccups.

Finally, finally, the movie ended. Before the credits began to roll, Rilla bolted for the exit. She didn't feel like chatting, even with Marcia or Kelly, who'd bruised her arm from jabbing it so many times.

"Earth!"

Stopping, Rilla squinted into the afternoon sunlight. Only one person called her that.

Joshua stepped from the theater and trotted after her. What was he coming to tell her? How much fun he had giggling in the dark with Tina?

Hiccup.

"Remember our deal?" He spoke in a hushed voice, like they were on a spy mission.

"Deal?"

"You know. How I get to play ball with Burly?"

"Oh."

Tina emerged from the theater. Her gaze fluttered about the crowd, landing on Joshua. Even this far away, Rilla could see her wrinkly frown.

Tina's displeasure gave Rilla confidence. She smiled at Joshua, maintaining eye contact. She laughed at everything he said. She even reached out and touched his arm. *(Thanks for the tips, Aunt Poppy.)*

"Do you want to come over *now* and play with Burly?" she asked, holding her breath to keep from hiccuping in his face.

"No." He glanced back at the theater. "I can't do it now."

Ah, he had plans.

"Hey, Josh!" Tina bellowed.

"What about tonight?" Joshua whispered. "We can smuggle Burly to Willow Park."

"What?! You mean take the monster out in public?"

"Yeah. After dark so no one will see him. We can play on the soccer field or the softball field. Lights won't be on; no games are played on Sunday nights."

"I—I don't know."

"Josh-u-a," Tina singsonged. "We're lea-ving."

Tina was waiting with Marcia and Andrew. Was this a double date?

"Gotta go. See you . . . a little after nine? Should be dark by then. Meet me at the dugout."

Rilla felt dazed. What had she just agreed to?

Unable to force her legs to move, she watched the foursome head toward the House of Sweets.

They didn't invite me because I'm an Earth, she reasoned. *Earths don't eat sweets.*

Rilla headed in the opposite direction—toward home and those who needed her and wanted her around.

So what if they were monsters?

Hiccup.

Back at Harmony House, Rilla hurried to the attic. Rushing inside, she slipped, catching hold of the doorknob to keep from falling.

Rilla peered at the floor. Puddles of water led from the bathroom to . . . "Chelsea!"

The mermaid was propped on a pillow in the rocking chair. She looked pale and glassy-eyed.

A few feet away, Burly tossed one ball after another to her.

Chelsea missed them all.

"What have you done?" Rilla dashed to rescue the mermaid. She looked pitiful. Her slick tail was drying out. Even the green was fading from her hair.

Snatching Chelsea from the chair, Rilla carried her into the bathroom and gently slid her into the tub.

Burly followed, chittering a guilty-sounding explanation.

After a few seconds, the mermaid's tail gave a tiny flip. Color rushed back into her face and hair. Diving under, she hid beneath the greenery.

"Bur-ly," Rilla moaned. "She can't survive out of water. You could've killed her."

Burly's paws flew to his face. He looked horrified.

Rilla's own words registered in her brain. How could he kill a monster who wasn't supposed to be alive in the first place?

"I'm sorry." She lifted him into her arms. He gave her a hug. It made her feel mushy and sentimental. "I know you just wanted to play."

The mermaid surfaced, shooting out of the water to her waist. She shook her hair, as if showing them she was fine.

Rilla breathed a sigh of relief, reaching to smooth tangly locks away from Chelsea's face.

Burly made a cheering sound. He was back to his bubbly self.

Clank, clank, clank!

Sparrow needed her downstairs.

Rilla quickly changed into jeans and a shirt, first because it might be chilly after dark in Willow Park and second because she didn't want Joshua to see her wearing the same clothes she'd worn to the movie—the clothes she'd worn when he took Tina out for dessert.

Burly approved of her evening attire by tweeting his whistle and giving her a bouncy ovation on the water bed.

Downstairs, Sparrow and Aunt Poppy served guests in the dining room. Rilla was stuck in the kitchen, helping Mother Lazuli put finishing touches on her weird lasagna dinner.

Rilla watched what she said around the kitchen clairvoyant. What she *wanted* to say was, *"Stop staring at me."* The woman's unrelenting gaze made her nervous. What was she looking for?

Rilla tore fresh parsley into tiny sprigs and garnished six salads. *Stop staring* became her mantra. Chanting it in her mind, she wondered if the plea was sinking into Mother Lazuli's consciousness.

Suddenly the woman stopped her vigorous chopping of leeks and put a hand to her forehead. "The first of the month," she proclaimed.

"Huh?" Rilla had no idea what she was talking about.

"A cloud hangs over your head, child," Mother L.

said. "Something will happen to you on the first of the month."

Rilla stepped to the refrigerator to peer at the calendar, held up by one of Sparrow's endangered species magnets. (A spotted owl.) Tuesday was June first. So what?

"I . . ." she began, then swallowed the rest of the sentence. The first of the month! Of course. The arrival of another monster. The June Selection of the Monster of the Month Club.

Rilla glanced at Mother Lazuli in amazement. *How could she know that? I wasn't even thinking about monsters.* Yikes.

Rilla returned to her parsley sprigs. *Geez, the woman is good. . . .*

"What were you going to say?" Mother L. demanded, whisking a butcher knife through the leeks with one fell swoop. "You can tell me."

Ha, right. "I was going to say, um, that the first of June means Father's Day is around the corner, and I, um, always feel sad on Father's Day."

Quick thinking, Earth. Throw her off track by bringing up another one of your problems.

Mother L. spooned a taste of wasabi sauce out of a bubbling pan. "Is that so?" she said, as though they were discussing the weather.

Rilla knew Mother Lazuli despised the man Sparrow had married. She wasn't sure why, but over the years, she'd caught bits and pieces of discussions about *HIM*. Discussions that ended abruptly the instant "the daughter" stepped into the room.

"Tell me about my father," Rilla blurted, hoping to lead the woman further from her truthful hunch about the first of the month.

"Puh," she answered. "Not much to say. How could a man leave his wife and unborn child?"

Precisely the question Rilla wanted answered.

Mother Lazuli resumed her scrutiny. "Something *else* is going to happen on the first of June," she began. "Something that will greatly affect you. And *I* think you know what it is."

Gulp. Too close for comfort. "Well, I—"

"Aloha!"

Mr. Tamerow burst into the kitchen, saving Rilla from further hedging.

"Look what I brought for your classroom. All the way from Hilo, Hawaii, my last destination." He unrolled a poster depicting a travel-worn earth, badly in need of repair. Underneath it read:

I'm 4 billion years old.
The least you could do is be kind to me.

Rilla laughed. Dropping the parsley, she whisked the poster out of Mr. Tamerow's hand and dashed into the classroom to hang it.

She was *not* going to worry about the June first

"cloud hanging over her head," *or* Tina's "date" with Joshua, *or* how she was supposed to show up at Willow Park with a monster in tow.

Right now, she was going to enjoy dinner at Harmony House with Mr. Tamerow and José—two of her favorite guests.

At least two out of three wasn't bad.

16

THE FORBIDDEN TOPIC

Rilla polished off her odd-tasting lasagna more out of politeness than hunger. Too bad she couldn't graze through cupboards later and fill up on junk. Ha. Junk never made it through the doors of Harmony House.

If it wasn't for the kittens, words like *Dorito* and *Oreo* would be extinct on the B & B acre.

Surprisingly, dessert was on the menu tonight—their annual birthday cake to honor the "Mother of Ecology," Rachel Carson, who waged a war in the 1950s against environmental pollutants, like pesticides.

She died long before Rilla was born, but Sparrow once heard the woman speak at a convention, and her "protect our world" philosophies made a big impression on the future owner of Harmony House. Obviously.

Dinner had almost been fun. José and Aunt Poppy batted witticisms back and forth, making everybody laugh. Even Mother Lazuli.

Aunt Poppy's hair was French braided, compliments of a hair stylist in suite G-8. Plus she wore a (rare) dress showing off the tan she'd acquired driving the Ride-a-Mower around the yard once a week.

Sparrow traded herbal health tips with Mr. Tamerow. (Such as, take blue vervain, bayberry, and yarrow at the first sign of a cold.) After that, Mr. T. brought them up to date on one of his recent trips—to Mérida on the Yucatán Peninsula.

Then Mother Lazuli read everyone's aura.

Normally Rilla would have died of embarrassment, but the group already knew the quirkiness of the blue woman. They listened attentively, whether or not they believed she could actually see their "life force" shimmering around them.

According to Mother L., José's musical career was destined for success, and Aunt Poppy was happy and in love (making her blush big time).

Sparrow was entering a new phase of her life, which would bring her "spiritual peace and closure from past events."

Mr. Tamerow was badly in need of a vacation from all his traveling, and Rilla, well, Rilla's aura had lots of red in it. Red meant anger.

Other than that, Mother L. said, "Secrets stored in

Rilla's heart would cause it to break if not shared with one she trusted."

Rilla pondered the woman's words. Did she really *know* all these things? Or had she cracked open too many Chinese fortune cookies?

Well, forget her angry aura. Rilla preferred to concentrate on the clock. She didn't want to be late for her rendezvous with Joshua.

After dinner, everyone carried mugs of cappuccino outside to the patio where the air was cooler. Rilla helped Sparrow clean the kitchen.

"Okay, little daughter with a red aura," her mother began. "With whom are you angry? Me? Or is it puberty in general?"

"What do you mean?"

"Well, I remember being angry at the world for at least three years when I was a teenager," Sparrow said. "Maybe it runs in the Earth family."

Pinowski family, Rilla corrected. "I'm not mad at you. Sometimes, I just get . . . angry . . . for a bunch of reasons."

"Does this have anything to do with the snippy *Promoting Harmony in Our Day-to-Day Lives* essay you wrote for your final exam?"

Rilla sighed. "Maybe."

"Go on."

She started to say, "Forget it; it's nothing." But instead, all kinds of issues spilled out of her mouth:

"I'm tired of the rules around here—like be quiet all the time. It's my house too. And, why do you embarrass me in front of the home-schoolers? You *never* defend me. *And,* why *can't* I take the kittens to my room? AND—WHY DON'T YOU EVER TALK TO ME ABOUT MY FATHER?"

Rilla's last question stopped her cold. Sure, it was constantly on her mind, but she hadn't meant to yell it out loud at her mother.

Sparrow had been listening intently, but when Rilla's voice crescendoed with the "father question," every bit of color drained from her face.

Uh-oh. The Forbidden Topic.

"You think about your father?" Sparrow asked in a quiet voice.

"Sure."

"Why?"

"Because I don't *know* him. And I want to. Why doesn't he ever call? Or come see me? And why won't you *talk* about him? To *me*?"

Sparrow dropped a dish towel and grasped the counter. "Whoa," she mumbled three times in a row.

Rilla bit her lip, surprised at how much anger was bottled up inside her over this topic. The *problem* with getting angry was that it made her feel like crying. She held her breath, not wanting to give in to tears and let her mother off the hook.

"First of all," Sparrow began. "The reason we fixed up the attic is so you'd have a place all to yourself. We respect your privacy. You can play tapes, your ukulele, or the radio to your heart's content up there, and it shouldn't bother guests.

"Second, I didn't know I embarrassed you in front of the home-schoolers. Tell me next time, okay?"

Rilla nodded. Sounded simple. Why hadn't *she* thought of it?

"And, maybe I don't rush to defend you in front of others because I want you to learn to defend yourself." Pausing, she gave Rilla a sad look. "You can't depend on someone else to save you."

Mmm. Was her mother speaking from personal experience?

"And, about the kittens, we can't bring them inside because a guest might be allergic. The cats love the barn; they're fine out there."

Rilla hated her mother's logical answers. They gave her nothing to argue against.

"And . . . your father." She said the word as though it tasted bittersweet. "I didn't know you felt this way. Maybe it's time we talked about him."

Picking up the dish towel, Sparrow scrunched it into a ball as if preparing herself for the worst. "Go ahead. Ask me anything."

Rilla glanced out the window. The sky was growing dark. She had to meet Joshua in a half hour.

"I—I can't think about it now. Can we have this talk another time?"

Sparrow visibly relaxed, tossing the towel onto the

table. "Absolutely. And Rill?" she added. "I'm sorry I've kept it such a secret. It's not something I've wanted to talk about, but he *is* your father and you have a right to know."

The espresso machine started to gurgle. Sparrow directed the steam jet into a cup of milk until the liquid became hot and frothy.

"Let's take our cappuccino outside with our guests."

"Um, I'd really rather go to my room, if it's okay."

"Fine. You don't want to hang around with a bunch of grown-ups. I understand. But please say good night first."

Rilla stepped outside while Sparrow sprinkled cinnamon on top of the froth in her mug.

Oreo and her kits were entertaining the group.

Scooping up Pepsi, Rilla knelt next to Mr. Tamerow's patio chair to listen in on the conversation. She scratched Pepsi's ear until soft purrs floated in the night air.

Mr. T. was holding Milk Dud. "Mother Lazuli is predicting my future," he said. His amazed grin resembled the cabbie's after she received Mother L.'s startling revelation about her life. "Guess what, Rilly? I might be married with children next time I visit."

He became so animated, Milk Dud sprang from his lap and scurried off into the bushes. "I'll have to rent the entire green floor to accommodate the size family Mother says I'm bound to have."

Everyone laughed except Rilla.

Already she was jealous of Mr. T.'s future kids. He'd
be too busy for her. He'd send *them* gifts from around
the globe instead of Rilla Harmony Earth. Or maybe
he'd take his kids with him on trips.

Rilla patted Pepsi away and bid everyone good night.
Hurrying inside, she ran up the back steps. She'd had
enough of Mother L.'s crazy prophecies for one night.
Especially if they promised to take Mr. Tamerow away
from her.

Shaking her head, she scolded herself for being silly.
It's just a prediction, Earth. Probably won't come true.

Rilla unlocked the door to the attic, feeling unsettled
about Sparrow answering her *missing father* questions.

So why didn't it make her happy after all these years
of waiting and wondering? Why, instead, did she feel
strangely sad? And nervous . . .

Right now, she didn't have time to ponder her future
conversation with Sparrow—or worry about Mr.
Tamerow's destiny.

The night wasn't over yet. She still had to figure out
a way to smuggle a live monster to Willow Park.

All because of her one true love.

17

MONSTER'S NIGHT OUT

Rilla tiptoed down the blue hallway and climbed out a side window leading to the fire escape. "Stop wiggling," she hissed at the pillowcase that held the squirming May monster.

Hoisting him under one arm, she slid the window shut, then tiptoed down the metal steps, being careful not to make too much noise and alert the group still chatting on the back patio.

The fire escape ended well above the ground. "I'm going to jump now," she warned Burly.

Thump-bump.

She landed in soft dirt in Sparrow's Dutch iris bed.

Burly spouted a chittery string of what sounded like monster curses.

"Sorry," she whispered.

Cutting across the front yard, Rilla slipped through

the privacy pines and headed down Hollyhock Road.

Headlights from a passing car flashed in her eyes as it rounded a curve. The car slowed.

Rilla sped up. How suspicious did she look?

She jogged three blocks to Willow Park. Dashing across the last street, she wound between trees and bushes bordering the park. In the distance, light from a full moon and streetlamps illuminated a lone figure standing next to the dugout on the ball field.

Her heart sped up at the sight of Joshua Banks waiting in the moonlight. Waiting for her, Rilla Harmony Earth.

The pounding of her heart kept time with punches from inside the pillowcase. She couldn't hold the monster much longer.

Twenty yards from the dugout, Burly's struggling paid off. The rubber band around the top of the pillowcase popped off, and the monster's scruffy head burst out.

He looked furious, whipping his head one way, then the other.

When he saw where he was, his anger melted. With a pleased gurgle, he began to fight his way out of the pillowcase.

Rilla dropped to one knee. "Okay, you can get out now. But stay with me." Suddenly she realized she should have brought a dog leash to keep him from running off. Of course she didn't *have* a dog leash, but surely Aunt Poppy had rope in the barn.

Burly dashed away.

"Hey!" Joshua called.

The monster froze, searching for the source of the shout.

In the dim light, a football came hurtling toward him.

Burly squealed with delight and dove for it, rolling over in the mud.

Rilla groaned. She hadn't thought about him getting dirty. She might have to throw him into the bathtub with Chelsea, clothes and all.

"You did it!" Joshua hollered, racing toward Rilla, a big grin on his face. His dimples were shadowed curves in the moonlight. "Come on."

The two trotted to the dugout with a monster on their heels.

Arranged on the bench were a soccer ball, a baseball, and a bat.

Joshua flipped the football into the air and caught it. "Okay, buddy, what do you want to play?"

The sports monster was beside himself. Snatching the soccer ball, he dashed onto the field.

Three players wasn't enough for a game, but it was enough for a hectic match of keep away.

After a while, Burly raced back for the bat and ball.

Rilla was better at softball. Batting and running she

enjoyed. Especially when the moon and streetlamps offered just enough light to make it look like she knew what she was doing.

Soon Burly was ready for football—not Rilla's favorite, especially since she already had scabs on both knees.

After being tackled twice by the monster, Rilla opted to sit out. She wouldn't have minded being tackled by Joshua, but he never tried. Sigh.

Rilla sat on the cool grass. If any passerby happened along, the scene on the field might look like a kid and a toddler playing ball.

From a distance, that is.

In the moonlight, Burly looked fairly normal, although he could run faster and jump higher than a real kid his size—plus, he was a lot hairier.

Joshua trotted over, falling onto the grass beside her. "This guy's wearing me out," he huffed.

"Don't you remember Bur's selection card?" she asked. "It said the May monster doesn't like to lose."

"No kidding."

Burly danced around them, tweeting his whistle, trying to drum up another round of soccer.

"No, please," Joshua groaned. "We'll play another night."

The disappointed monster finally gave up. Circling the field, he collected the bat and balls, dumping them next to Joshua.

"Thanks, buddy." Joshua sighed and closed his eyes.

"Hey." Rilla jabbed him gingerly in the side. "Don't fall asleep. We have to get home before curfew."

"Oh, right." Joshua squinted at his watch, but didn't move.

"Hey, look," he said, returning the nudge. "The stars have come out."

Rilla leaned back to gaze at the heavens. The moon had been swallowed by a monstrous cloud, allowing stars to reveal themselves. She tried to make out lightning-shaped patterns over Harmony House's neighborhood, but far too many stars dotted the blackness.

The majesty of the night sky was breathtaking. Rilla couldn't believe she was actually sitting here in Willow Park, stargazing with Joshua Banks. If someone had told her six months ago she'd be doing this, she would have told them they were crazy.

One good thing about the monsters—they'd won her Joshua's attention. That made them worth the aggravation, didn't it . . . ?

She glanced at her one true love. He was staring at her.

Rilla's temperature shot up three hundred degrees. "What?"

"Thanks for bringing Burly tonight. I had a great time. He's really good. I mean, he's better at sports than Andrew and Wally."

Why couldn't Joshua's "great time" be credited to

her? "He was born, um, I mean, *made* to play sports," she told him.

"Should we take Chelsea swimming at the pool tomorrow?"

Rilla gaped at him. Was he joking? His grin told her he was. "Yeah, right," she said.

They fell silent, watching the glittery sky. Rilla wanted the night to go on and on and never end. But city curfew was drawing near. And she still had to figure out a way to smuggle Burly back into Harmony House.

Could she reach the fire escape? Why hadn't she made sure before racing off to the park?

Burly. He was being awfully quiet.

Rilla sat up. The monster was nowhere in sight.

"Ohmigosh!"

She sprang to her feet.

"What?" Joshua scrambled to stand beside her.

"Burly!" Rilla shouted, scanning the field.

No familiar chitter met her ears.

Without wasting a minute, she and Joshua launched a monster hunt.

Burly wasn't in the dugout, on either field, or in the surrounding bushes.

Rilla ran, frantically looking behind every tree and rock until Joshua caught up and grabbed her arm.

"Stop," he told her. "It's no use. We've searched the entire park. Three times."

Rilla swallowed hard to keep from crying in front of him. The fear and concern on his face surely matched hers.

All she could think about was innocent little Burly. Alone in the world. He was her responsibility, and she'd *lost* him.

What have I done?

"He's gone," she whispered in a shaky voice. "He's really, really gone."

18

A STRANGE HAIRY KID ON THE LOOSE

Rilla lay in bed staring at the ceiling fan as it hummed away in the shadows of early dawn.

Burly had been gone one whole day. And two nights.

Where *was* he? She felt so responsible, like a mother who'd misplaced her child.

Was he all right? *Please be all right,* she begged the ceiling fan.

Even Chelsea knew Burly was gone. She must have gotten used to their games of catch. Her trilling cries sounded an awful lot like she was calling someone.

Calling Burly to come play.

Rilla missed him as much as the mermaid did. The monsters were her own little attic family, and it didn't seem right with one absent.

The only advantage to having a missing monster was that Joshua Banks called every few hours, checking to see if new clues to Burly's whereabouts had surfaced.

Rilla loved the attention, even though it had meant major teasing from José and Aunt Poppy.

Joshua had helped her search. Plus, they'd monitored the news on TV and radio—in case anyone reported a strange hairy kid on the loose.

But no one had reported anything of the kind.

Was Burly smart enough to keep himself hidden?

Or had someone kidnapped him?

Were they selling him to a circus this very minute? To star as a sideshow attraction?

The image of Burly doing silly tricks for a circus crowd made Rilla pull the quilt over her head and moan.

Getting out of bed this morning was difficult. One, because of Burly, and two, because Mr. Tamerow and José had both departed.

José had gone to another gig in Florida, and Mr. T. was off to a business meeting in Kabul, which was somewhere in Afghanistan, which was somewhere in Asia, which was a long way from Harmony House.

How could Mr. T. breeze in and out before she had a chance to tell him everything? Maybe *he* knew how to find a missing monster, only now it was too late to ask. He was already winging his way across the Atlantic.

One more problem kept Rilla in bed.

Today was June first.

Something was waiting for her down at the community mailboxes.

Something alive and peculiar. A new monster.

Yikes.

Pulling back the quilt, she glanced at the clock. Almost nine. If she didn't go after the mail soon, Sparrow might go get it herself, which she sometimes did when Rilla was slow.

If her mother found a wiggly box in the mail, the monster secret would definitely be out.

Above the sound of Chelsea's lonely trilling, Rilla heard the muffled ring of the telephone. She counted to five.

Clank, clank, clank.

It was for her.

She didn't have a phone in her room, but she'd borrowed one of the cordless guest phones from the third-floor landing. Sitting up, she lifted it off her dresser. "Hello?"

"It's me."

Her one true love.

Rilla leaned against a pillow. If only he were calling to ask about *her* instead of—

"Have you found him yet?"

"No." She sighed. "I watched the eleven-o'clock news last night. Not a word about monster sightings in the neighborhood."

"Well, I'm heading out on my bike to look some more. I'll stop by later."

"Today's June first," Rilla blurted before he hung up.

"So?"

"Another monster will be moving into my attic today."

"No kidding?" His voice sounded breathless with excitement. "When?"

"I'm on my way to the mailbox right now. Well, *almost* now," she added, glancing at her pajamas.

"I'll be right over."

The phone clicked in her ear.

Joshua's imminent arrival shoved her out of bed. She dressed in record time, barely stopping to scold Chelsea for overflowing the tub again.

Rilla flew downstairs, grabbed the mailbag off a hook by the sideboard, and started down Hollyhock Road to the mailboxes.

Halfway there, Joshua zoomed around a curve on his bike, skidding to a sideways stop beside her. Hopping off, he gave her his two-day-old frown. "You okay, Earth?"

She shrugged.

"This is all my fault," he began.

"No, it's not."

"I talked you into taking Burly outdoors."

"I should have been watching him."

"You didn't know he would run away."

"He's got to come back for food. Who else knows to give him baseball cards and golf tees and Cracker Jacks?"

This was the same conversation they'd had yesterday. Twice. At least talking to Joshua Banks was getting easier.

At the mailboxes, Rilla opened the one marked EARTH.

"Is it there?" Joshua's whisper was full of anticipation.

Rilla pulled out the B & B's mail and dumped it into the cloth bag.

Next, with trembling hands, she slid out a large cardboard box and peered at the label:

M.O.T.M. CLUB
Castelo Branco, Portugal

"Wow," Joshua murmured. "Portugal."

"Hey, what's going on?" came a grumbly voice.

Rilla jumped, almost dropping the monster box.

Tina studied the two of them with narrowed eyes.

"Hi, Welter," Joshua exclaimed.

Rilla cringed. Why'd he have to sound so darn friendly, and why'd he have to call Tina by *her* last name, too?

Disgusted, she tried to hide the box, but it was too big.

Tina pointed at it. "What's that?"

"Um, nothing."

Tina scoffed. "People mail you *nothing* in a great big

box? Oh, yeah, I forgot. Anything crazy can happen when it comes to the Earth family."

Joshua pretended a sudden interest in the overhanging willow branches.

Rilla figured he'd rather remain neutral. Slamming the mailbox, she handed him the bag so she could carry the monster box with both hands.

"Let's go." She'd tried to say it in a normal voice, but it sounded bossy, the way Tina might say it, which made Rilla shoot Joshua a look of apology.

Fifteen reactions hit Tina's face at the same time, making it contort in an unflattering sort of way.

"Go?" she blurted. "Where are you going?"

"Home." Rilla loved befuddling her.

Joshua flipped his bike around.

"Hey, Josh, wanna ride bikes down the river path?"

His gaze returned to the incredibly interesting willow branches. "Naw. Not now. Maybe later."

Tina's mouth actually fell open.

Rilla swallowed a monster grin.

"Are you going with *her*?" Tina hissed.

Joshua shrugged. "Yeah, why not?"

Now Tina didn't know *how* to react. "Well, um, can I come?"

NO! Rilla shouted in her mind. She beamed her message so furiously at Joshua's brain, she was surprised his left ear didn't burst into flames.

"Gosh, Welter, you probably wouldn't want to."

Swinging a leg over his bike, he shoved off to make a fast getaway.

"Why not?" Tina's voice was snarly.

"We're working on our summer projects," Rilla told her. *Brilliant, Earth.*

Before Tina could remind her that *she* had a summer project too, Rilla bolted after Joshua.

Tina's comments were lost to the wind as Rilla raced down Hollyhock Road. She hated jostling the box, but putting a quick distance between herself and Tina was more important.

Rilla slipped through the privacy pines while Joshua took the long way around on his bike. Peeking back between the trees, she scouted the street to make sure Tina hadn't followed them.

Score one for me.

Chuckling, she raced across the lawn. She, Rilla Harmony Earth, had just won Joshua Banks's attention away from crabby Tina Welter.

Sometimes the universe *was* fair.

19

AN UNINVITED GUEST

"There you are!" exclaimed Sparrow the instant Rilla stepped through the double oak doors into Harmony House. "Where've you *been*?"

"Getting the mail," Rilla answered, feeling defensive. Joshua lifted the mailbag to prove she was right.

Please don't embarrass me in front of him, she pleaded silently.

Sparrow gave a quick nod to Joshua and hurried on. "Ninety things have gone wrong this morning; I desperately need your help."

Rilla hoped her mother was exaggerating.

Casually setting the monster box on the sideboard, Rilla took the bag from Joshua, dumped out the mail, and hung the bag on its hook.

Act normal and she won't ask about the box.

"Three guests have called to complain about a dog

upstairs. A *dog*," Sparrow rasped. "Heaven knows how it got inside. One guest said it looked like *two* dogs. I don't have time to chase it down, and Poppy took José to the airport and never came back, so will you *please* go find the animal and get it out of here?"

"Sure." Sounded easy. Rilla swooped the box under one arm and started up the stairs.

"Not only that," Sparrow continued. "The guest in the suite beneath your room claims water is leaking from the ceiling."

Water? Chelsea! Ohmigosh!

Sparrow clasped a hand to her forehead the way people in TV headache commercials do. "I've called the Tonkawa sisters, and they're coming to fix the leak."

"B-but it's my fault," Rilla stammered. "I accidentally filled the tub too full. The sisters don't need to come, I—"

"Please." Sparrow held up her other hand. "Just leave the attic door unlocked so they can get in."

The thought of the Tonkawa sisters storming her bathroom made Rilla feel faint—which is what the sisters might do when they discovered a live mermaid swimming in the tub. "When are they coming?"

Sparrow began to rummage through drawers in the registration desk. "I couldn't pin them down; this is their busy season. Air conditioners tend to break when people need them most, according to Lottie."

Sparrow slammed a drawer, exasperated. "On top of

everything else, I've lost my bottle of kelp. It was with my chlorella and spirulina; I don't know how it could've disappeared."

Rilla gulped. She'd meant to take a few capsules and return the bottle to the cabinet, but Burly's disappearance had thrown off her life.

Sparrow gave up her search, eyeing Joshua as if trying to decide what the heck he was doing here.

"We're planning our summer projects," Rilla said. That explanation had worked on Tina; maybe it would work on her mother, too.

"Fine." Sparrow gave Joshua a tired smile. "Stay for lunch, if you'd like."

Rilla winced. *Please don't offer him leftover sushi lasagna.*

"Thank you, Ms. Earth," he said.

"Come on." Rilla headed upstairs. *How could I be so lucky? Sparrow didn't mention the—*

"What's in the box?" her mother called.

Both Rilla and her heart stalled on the first landing.

Before she could answer, her mother added, "Oh, it's June; I'll bet it's one of those stuffed toys, isn't it? The ones Abe is having sent to you."

Rilla opened her mouth, but nothing came out.

The stunned look on Joshua's face reminded her that *he* didn't know her *mom* knew. Well, her mom knew about Mr. Tamerow's gift, but she didn't know the monsters were *real*.

Sparrow pulled a pair of scissors from the desk drawer and handed them up to her. "Let's have a look at it."

Rilla's hand trembled as she took the scissors. Her mind warped toward the speed of light, looking for a reason *not* to open the monster box.

"So, Ms. Earth," Joshua began in a chipper voice. "What are those ninety things that have gone wrong this morning?"

"My rolls!" Sparrow yelped. "Thanks for reminding me." Skirting the registration desk, she dashed down the hall. "Make that ninety-*one* if my dinner rolls burn!"

"Thankyouthankyouthankyou," Rilla gushed.

Joshua grinned. "Let's go open the box in private."

She and Joshua hurried upstairs. At the end of the blue floor, they started up the narrow attic steps.

A whine met Rilla's ears. Something loomed at the top.

"The dog!" Joshua exclaimed.

Rilla forced her eyes to adjust to the dim stairwell. Joshua was right. A dog hunched on the top step.

Something sat beside it.

A monster.

"Burly!" Rilla hissed. "You've come home!"

Joshua took the steps two at a time. "Hey, buddy."

Rilla followed, quickly unlocking the attic door so they could whisk the furry fugitives out of view. Carefully she set the M.O.T.M. Club box on her desk, then turned her attention to Burly.

He was a mess: muddy shorts, tangly fur, raggedy holes in his shirt. Rilla didn't know whether to hug him or scold him, but boy, was she glad to have him back.

With him was a pitiful-looking mongrel with lentil-colored fur as matted as the monster's and eyes that melted Rilla's heart. She petted him. He didn't look full grown, yet he was bigger than Burly.

The dog licked Rilla's hand, then bounded away to explore the attic.

She liked him. A whole lot more than she liked Burly right now.

Rilla grabbed the monster's arm to keep him from dashing off to play with the dog. "Why did you run away? And how could you march into the B & B and let people *see* you?" she added, glad he'd been mistaken for a dog.

Rilla didn't expect an explanation. Still, Burly raised a paw and babbled a long excuse. Sounded like a good one, too, if only Rilla could understand what he said.

Chelsea began to call her monster friend.

Rilla released his arm. "Go," she told him.

With an excited squeal, Burly dashed into the bathroom to tell the mermaid of his adventures on the "outside."

Rilla still had Chelsea to deal with. How could she make the mermaid keep water *inside* the tub?

Too many problems demanded her immediate attention.

First things first. She'd better get Burly's new pet outside. And fast, before Sparrow came unglued.

Joshua was having a great time playing chase with the dog. "He might be hungry, Earth. Can we feed him?"

"We've got to get *rid* of him, remember? My mom's orders."

Still, Rilla tossed one of Burly's balls to the dog. He tumbled head over heels, racing to catch it.

She giggled at his antics. How weak her heart was when it came to creatures—stuffed or real.

He didn't have a collar, so Joshua grasped him gently by the scruff of the neck and led him to the door.

Burly zoomed out of the bathroom and blocked their path. Holding out both arms, he vigorously shook his head.

"Oh?" Rilla said, interpreting. "You think he belongs to you? And you want to keep him?"

A snippy monster argument ensued.

Rilla couldn't translate everything, but she got the gist of it. And the more they tried to get the dog out the door, the more Burly made it clear that either his new friend stayed in the attic or *he* went outside with the dog.

"Rill!" came Sparrow's voice up the stairs. "Did you find the beast?"

"Yes!" Rilla called back, resisting the urge to tell her how *many* beasts she'd found.

"Well, then, get him out of here. Poppy's taking her own sweet time getting back from the airport. I may need you if she doesn't get home before checkout time."

At checkout time, the entry hall was crowded with departing guests finalizing their bills. Both Earth sisters were on duty then.

"What are we going to do?" Joshua asked. "Burly's *not* going to part with the mutt, and your mom will know if we don't take him outside."

The dog barked. The noise echoed loudly in the stairwell.

Joshua was right. No way could they hide a barking dog in the attic.

That left only one solution. .

Rilla grabbed her standby pillowcase. "Put Burly into this. Take him out the side window and down the fire escape. I'll take the dog out the back so my mom can see me following her orders. Meet me inside the barn. Burly and his pet can stay there—if the dog doesn't mind kittens."

Rilla knew her plan was risky. What if she lost Burly again?

This time the monster went into the pillowcase without a struggle, as if he understood her strategy.

After showing Joshua how to get to the fire escape, Rilla headed downstairs with the dog, hoping he was a stray so she could keep him.

Earth, you know better than that.

She ignored her inner voice, cooing to the dog. She was already as attached to the scruffy mutt as she was to all the monsters who arrived at Harmony House in boxes.

Boxes! Rilla froze in midstep.

The monster box! She hadn't opened it!

In all the confusion of finding Burly and the dog, she'd completely forgotten about the arrival of the June monster.

Should she go back?

Arf! Yip yip—woof!

"RILLA HARMONY EARTH!" came Sparrow's frazzled shout.

Urging the dog downstairs, Rilla avoided her mother's eyes, scooting past her as quickly as possible, escorting the uninvited guest out the door.

Perhaps, Rilla reasoned, if the June monster had survived in its cardboard home all the way from Portugal, maybe it could wait a few minutes longer.

She hoped her earthly logic worked in the monster world.

20
UNUSUAL
VIBRATIONS

Rilla hurried the dog to the barn. Before she was halfway across the yard, she'd chosen a name for him: Taco.

He'd fit right in with her junk-food cats.

Naming him is serious business. It means you want to keep him.

I do want to keep him. And so does Burly.

What will Sparrow say?

Rilla didn't know what Sparrow would say, and she wasn't in the mood to think about it right now.

Inside the barn, Burly was having a heyday, playing chase with Milk Dud and Pepsi. As his pudgy legs climbed the ladder to the loft, the kittens scampered up their own way—hopping from the bench of Aunt Poppy's weight machine to the top of a cabinet, then to the soft hay in the loft.

With a happy yip, the dog tore from Rilla's grasp to join the race. He wasn't as graceful as the cats—slipping and sliding on the cabinet before his final leap.

"We should name him," Joshua said.

"I already did." Rilla felt pleased that she and her one true love shared the same idea.

The dog woofed at the kittens.

"Hush up, Taco! Sparrow might hear you."

"Taco?" Joshua laughed. "Excellent choice."

The dog began to nip at cat tails.

Then Burly did something strange. He clicked his tongue, led the dog away, and yammered at him in monster language.

The dog whined, nuzzled Burly, then lay down and calmly let the cats creep up to sniff, inspect—and accept him.

"Wow, did you see that?" Joshua stepped up the ladder for a better view. "Burly can talk to the dog. They understand each other."

Joshua's praise made Rilla feel like a proud mother. She'd suspected the monsters were a whole lot smarter than she'd first given them credit for.

"Lunchtime!"

Rilla cringed. Why did Sparrow have to yell announcements out the back door? It was so humiliating.

She glanced at Joshua. "Um, do you want to stay for lunch?" She figured he'd say no to avoid a second dose of her mother's rotten mood.

Joshua acted unsure. "I should go home. My grandparents are visiting."

"Oh."

"I slipped out this morning to look for Burly, but now that he's back. . . ."

Joshua's voice trailed off. Rilla wondered if it meant he wouldn't be coming over as often.

"Hey," he exclaimed. "If Burly stays in the barn, I can sneak in and play ball with him anytime, right? Without disturbing your family."

Rilla nodded. *He wants to play with Burly by himself, Earth, not with you tagging along.* She tried to act as if it didn't matter.

After Joshua left, Rilla found a long section of rope and tied Taco to the Ride-a-Mower. She hated tying him up, but how else could she keep the door open for the cats and keep him—and Burly—inside the barn? She knew Burly would stay with Taco. After the fit he pitched, why wouldn't he?

Maybe Joshua could help her install one of those swinging pet doors so the kittens could go in and out and Taco could have the run of the barn. In the afternoons, she'd take him to Willow Park to play, and on days that she couldn't, Joshua would take him.

How's Aunt Poppy going to mow the lawn with a dog tied to the Ride-a-Mower?

Rilla groaned. Sooner or later, she'd be caught hiding the dog in the barn. Then what? She smiled to herself.

I'll do what Burly did. Give them the ol' "If he goes, I go" ultimatum. . . .

Rilla left the barn door open just enough for a cat to slip through. *I suppose*, she said to herself, *I'll worry about getting caught when it happens.*

Satisfied, she wandered across the yard, making a quick check of her science project anemometers. They were still working. The paper cups caught the mild breeze, rotating slowly. According to the meters, wind speed was six miles per hour.

Inside, Sparrow was alone in the kitchen making sandwiches. Aunt Poppy's purse was on the counter, but she was nowhere in sight.

Rilla put two and two together. The Earth sisters had quarreled.

She tiptoed toward the back stairs as quietly as possible. The still-in-the-box monster waiting in the attic tugged at her conscience. For better or worse, she had to unleash it.

"Stop," Sparrow commanded.

Rats.

"Eat before you go running off."

Rilla sent mental apologies to the June monster. A few more minutes wouldn't hurt, would it?

"Isn't Joshua staying for lunch?"

"No. He had to go home."

Sparrow set avocado and bean sprout sandwiches on the table. A lock of hair had come loose from her poofy band. With her hair in disarray and the troubled expression on her face she looked so forlorn, Rilla felt sorry for her.

On the spur of the moment, she hugged her mom. "I'm sorry you're in a bad mood today. What else has gone wrong?"

Sparrow returned the hug, pleasantly surprised by the unexpected concern. "Just a bunch of silly things. I need to hire extra help this summer—if we can afford it."

"Where's Mother Lazuli? Can't she help?"

Sparrow gestured toward the classroom. "She's lying down. Says she's getting unusual vibrations from Harmony House. They're giving her a queen-size headache."

"Unusual vibrations?"

Sparrow seemed reluctant to explain. "She thinks a few guests moved in without registering, although I can't imagine how that could possibly happen."

Rilla took her seat, biting into a sandwich in an effort to remain nonchalant. She could think of *four* guests who hadn't registered.

"Mother even knew the dog was in the house before the guests called to complain. She *really* has a powerful gift."

A million snide remarks begged to be uttered, but Rilla stifled them.

Sparrow fixed another sandwich and joined her at the table. "Since this is such a hectic day and I'm not getting help from Aunt You-Know-Who, maybe you could do *one* task that needs to be done."

Rilla wondered what Sparrow and Aunt You-Know-Who had argued about. José? Taking her "own sweet time" getting home from the airport? Her lovesickness?

Polishing off the sandwich, Rilla started to chug her juice, choking when she tasted it. Prune juice—yuck. The refrigerator was always full of prune juice when Mother Lazuli came to stay.

When Sparrow wasn't looking, Rilla dumped the juice down the sink and poured a glass of purified spring water from the jug in the refrigerator. "What do you want me to do?"

"Write an ad for the paper. Free kittens. Word it any way you want."

Horrified, Rilla backed away from the table and flattened herself against the pantry door. "No. No. No!"

Sparrow flinched at her strong reaction. "Excuse me?"

Rilla felt her lip quivering. "You can't give away my kittens."

"Why not? It's time to find them good homes."

"No."

Sparrow peered at her the way she did when she suspected Rilla was coming down with an illness. "We have four cats. That's three too many."

"But they don't bother anybody. I feed and take care of them, and—"

"No, they don't, and yes, you do. But I never intended to adopt a cat in the first place. If you recall, the mama cat adopted us. Had I known she was pregnant at the time, I wouldn't have given her room and board."

Sparrow didn't know the mama cat's name was Oreo. Mentioning it now would only start another argument since Sparrow didn't believe in naming animals. (She thought it might limit them from all nature intended them to be.)

Rilla balled her hands into fists. "You let the mama cat stay, and now the babies are our responsibility. We can't desert them."

"Ohhhhhhhh." Sparrow stopped dipping her un-bleached tea bag into a mug bearing the logo

Love Your Mother
(Earth)

She studied her only daughter. "*I* know what this is all about. This has nothing to do with the kittens at all, does it, Rill? This is about your father."

Rilla hadn't made the connection as quickly as Sparrow.

"Sooooo." Sparrow sighed. "I guess it's time to have our little talk."

Rilla grasped a chair to steady herself—and to squelch an overwhelming urge to bolt from the kitchen and run away—far from the look her mother was giving her right now.

21

THE MISSING-
FATHER STORY

Sparrow shoved plates away, squeezed raw honey into her mug of yellow dock tea, and made Rilla join her at the table.

Rilla sat stiffly on the edge of a chair, confused about why she'd rather be anyplace else on earth except here with Sparrow—now that all those questions, buried deep in her heart for thirteen years, were about to be answered.

In spite of the heat emanating from the berry banana cake baking in the oven, she hugged herself, shivering in anticipation of the story she'd waited her whole life to hear. The Missing-Father story.

Sparrow fiddled with her tea so long, Rilla wanted to yell at her.

Finally her mother began. "Your father and I met at a protest rally against a nuclear power plant. After that, we were together every day. He was the first guy I'd met who shared my passionate concern for the planet."

Sparrow shot Rilla a pained look, as though wishing she could end the story right there.

But Rilla was determined to hear her out, even though dread and anticipation coiled inside her stomach.

"We married far too soon, and took off for India in search of our own truths." She gave a sad chuckle. "I—we—were so naive in those days. But it was all very wonderful. After India, we traveled the globe, as Abe would say, stopping to work whenever we needed money.

"When we found out *you* were on the way, we came home so you'd be born in America." Sparrow stared at the ceiling, lost in thought, like it had been a long time since she'd allowed herself to recall the past.

"As soon as we stopped living as nomads and settled down to permanent jobs, the mystique of our unique life faded away." Sparrow's lip quivered. "Your father left to continue his search without me."

Rilla wanted to comfort her mother, yet panic closed her throat. Sparrow had just confirmed her deepest, darkest fear.

"So," she said in a breathy voice. "*I'm* the reason he left." She'd always suspected it was her fault, but hearing it wounded her deeply.

"Oh, *no.*" Sparrow reached across the table to grasp her hand. "It wasn't you; don't ever think that. Your father was thrilled with the news about you. It's just. . . . well . . . I exaggerate. In my mind, it was all wonderful, living free and without responsibility. Someone would mention a city that sounded intriguing, so we'd pack up and go there. One time, we even let the direction the wind was blowing tell us which way to travel."

Rilla watched years fall away from her mother's face as she became animated, caught up with her own story. This was a side of Sparrow she'd never seen. Traveling the way the wind blows? Her down-to-earth mother?

"There were problems long before I found out about you. Somewhere in Morocco, I knew it wouldn't last. We had a wonderful friendship, but the fact remained, we'd rushed it into a marriage."

Sparrow squeezed her hand. "It wasn't meant to be, Rill; you have to let him go."

How can I let him go when I've never known him? "What was he like?" she asked instead. Sparrow folded her hands on the table and stared at them. "He . . . he had this way of tugging on his beard when he spoke. And he *never* wore socks." She chuckled, as though the memory surprised her. "No matter where in the world we went, he always found a fresh flower for my hair. Every day, summer or winter."

Rilla hung on every word. Details. That's what she wanted. Details.

"And he used to steal my jokes and finish my sentences, and . . . oh, wait, I'll *show* you what he was like." Standing, Sparrow rummaged through a cabinet and drew out a manila envelope. "Everything in here is yours to keep."

Rilla peeked into the envelope. Besides pictures there were scribbled notes on matchbooks, a peace symbol on a leather string, pins from exotic-sounding places, and other bits and pieces from her father's life.

With trembling hands, Rilla pulled out photos of a young man with longish hair, a beard, flared jeans, and sandals. He was handsome—smiling in every picture, holding hands with a younger, thinner, more sparkly Sparrow.

"You have your father's—"

"Nose," Rilla said, noticing a familiar bony bump.

Sparrow laughed. "And his smile, plus many of his expressions. It's hard for me to forget him when I look at you and see his face."

Mmm. It surprised her that Sparrow still thought of him.

There was one more question Rilla needed to ask, but it scared her so badly, her voice quivered when she tried to get the words out. "Do you think he will ever come looking for me?"

Sparrow's face crinkled in guilt. Stalling, she sipped her tea. "I truly believed he might pop up on my doorstep one day to meet you. He was in love with the idea of having a child. And Rill, he'd be so proud of you; I'm sure of it. But . . . I probably made it difficult for him to find us—changing our name and moving across the country to buy Harmony House with Poppy."

The Pinowski-Earth name change had always haunted Rilla. Maybe when she grew up, she'd take back her birth name.

"So, it's not like your father never *tried* to visit you. He probably did."

Wow. Words to ponder for a long, long time.

Sparrow stood, ending the conversation. "Now you know the story—and you have the pictures to prove it." She gave a weak laugh, then kissed Rilla on the cheek. "I'm sorry this has hurt you; I never intended it to." She blotted her eyes. "Now, about the kittens. If we keep them, they'll have to be fixed, which cost me seventy dollars for the mama cat."

Rilla quickly figured the vet bill in her head, then groaned. "Three cats would cost over two hundred dollars?"

"Right . . . well, no. Males are cheaper to neuter."

"Why?" The instant the question slipped out of her mouth, Rilla was mortified. Obviously it had to do with the *location* of reproductive organs.

"It's a simpler procedure for male cats." Her mother grimaced at her as though thinking, *Do we have to have THAT talk today, too?*

Sparrow scribbled on a newspaper with a pencil. "Two males and one female would cost about a hundred and fifty dollars. That's a lot, Rill, and if I have to hire extra help this summer—"

"*I'll* work for you," she interrupted. "For free. My salary can go toward the vet bill." Rilla clutched the manila envelope to her chest, hoping it might convince Sparrow that she owed her daughter a few acts of kindness after the lifelong trauma she'd caused. "Please?"

"Fine. But it needs to be done ASAP, or we'll have more kittens on our hands, and I *cannot*—"

"I'll get right on it." Rilla gave her mom a snappy salute. "It will be my first official job as your new employee."

Sparrow's face softened into a grin—something Rilla rarely saw these days. "Thanks, kid." She playfully nudged Rilla on the chin. "So, why are you still sitting here? Get to work."

Rilla dashed upstairs. Working for her mother was the *last* way she wanted to spend her summer vacation. Yet if it meant keeping the kittens, then so be it. *Hooray!*

As Rilla neared the attic, she suddenly remembered what waited inside.

The June monster.

All her happiness over the kitten victory leaped to its death. Rilla couldn't *believe* she'd kept the monster waiting this long.

Sometimes monsters hold grudges.

"Hush," she rasped, scolding her unrelenting inner voice. "Now that I'm the mother of four cats, one dog, and six monsters, they'll all have to wait their blinkin' turn. . . ."

22

MONSTER
NUMBER THREE

Rilla pounded up the back steps. As she reached the blue floor, something caught her eye: a flash of turquoise. Disappearing down the main stairway.

Mother Lazuli! Rilla's neck heated. What was she doing this close to the attic? Snooping?

"I thought she was sick in bed," Rilla muttered. Had the woman gone sleuthing again? Searching for the cause of her *unusual vibrations*? Uh-oh.

Rilla stepped up the narrow stairwell. The attic door was unlocked.

Her heart zoomed into high gear.

Then she remembered. Sparrow had asked her to leave the door open for the Tonkawa sisters.

Good thing they hadn't shown up yet. *That* would be a disaster.

Wait a minute. Had Mother L. been *inside* the attic?

Of course not, her mind reasoned. *Why would she spy on you? She was probably in Aunt Poppy's room trying to smooth things over between the Earth sisters.*

Pleased with her logical explanation, Rilla focused on the problems at hand: figuring out a way to hide Chelsea and clean the rocks and greenery out of the tub. Ugh. Then she'd have to put it all back.

The M.O.T.M. Club box was where she'd left it, although it wouldn't have surprised her if the monster had ripped its way to freedom and taken over the attic the same way Icicle had done.

Rilla placed the manila envelope in the bottom drawer beneath her cookie tin. Later, she'd study the pictures and think about Sparrow's story.

Especially the parts like: *Your father was thrilled with the news about you.* And: *He was in love with the idea of having a child.* And: *It's not like he never tried to visit you. He probably did.*

Oh, how good those words sounded.

Rilla closed the dresser drawer and quietly sat at her desk.

It was time.

Finding a pair of scissors, she gingerly snipped the mailing tape off the package from Portugal.

Nothing in her life compared to the buzz she experienced unwrapping each new monster box. The contents were always a mystery.

Opening one end, she waited for something to leap out at her.

Nothing happened.

Rilla peeked inside. Fur the color of a June sky pleased her eyes.

She helped the monster out of the box.

This one was arriving the same way Chelsea, Burly, and Shamrock had arrived. Stuffed. Lifeless. A harmless toy.

Relief flooded through her.

So. She didn't have to worry about monster number three. (Or six, depending on how she counted.)

The June monster had wings, a pink beak, and yellow claws. Beady eyes stared back at her with no spark of life behind their glassy gaze.

Rilla shook the box until the announcement card fell out:

Monster of the Month Club

June Selection

Name: Summer   *Gender:* Female

Homeland: Portugal

Likes: Sunflower seeds, cola, worms

Needs plenty of room to exercise her wings

"Wow." Rilla was glad this one wasn't alive. Cola and sunflower seeds were easy. But worms? She'd have to dig up the backyard by flashlight and collect the slimy things in a jar.

Joshua Banks would do it for you.

"Oh, darn." A lost opportunity for Joshua to visit. "Too bad you're *not* real," she told Summer.

Noises from the bathroom broke her attention. Once again, in her early morning rush, she'd forgotten to feed poor Chelsea. The monster sounded angry—and rightfully so.

Rilla hugged her newest selection in the M.O.T.M. Club, admiring her blue feathery fur. She gave Summer a place of honor on the pillow between a walrus and an alligator.

Riffling through her underwear drawer, Rilla grabbed a tin of tuna and the can opener she'd snitched from the pantry.

When she stepped into the bathroom, shock stopped her at the door. The can opener slipped from her hand and clattered onto the tile.

Hunched over the hole where water pipes disappeared beneath the floor was a woman wearing orange overalls and an oversize tool belt.

23

NIGHTMARE IN THE TUB TALE

"Find anything yet?" hollered a voice from the attic stairwell.

Aunt Poppy burst into the bathroom.

"There you are!" she exclaimed. "Look at this tub, young lady. You have a lot of explaining to do."

The Tonkawa sister stood. According to her name tag, she was Dottie, the nice one.

Thank heavens for small favors. Rilla didn't think she was up to dealing with Lottie today.

"Can't find a single leak," Dottie said. "Pipes are fine, and the tub's as solid as a rock; they don't make 'em like this anymore." She clunked a wrench against the side to prove her point. "Looks like it overflowed, that's all."

Dottie pointed her wrench at Rilla. "Are you doing a science project in the tub?"

Rilla forced a smile, pretending to agree.

Chelsea is hiding under the greenery. If Dottie pulls the plug, they'll see her when the water drains.

Dottie and Aunt Poppy leaned over the bathtub, evaluating Rilla's ambitious attempt to re-create the Caribbean Sea surrounding Aruba.

"Go on downstairs," Rilla urged in a chipper voice. "I'll clean this up." She acted as if the tub's strange contents were as normal as dust under the bed. "Sorry you had to make a service call for no reason, Dottie."

"Still have to charge you, love. And you'll need to call a drywaller to fix the water damage on the third-floor ceiling. Not my expertise."

Rilla held the door open so the two could leave.

"Not so fast, young lady."

Her aunt's staccato command made Rilla want to drop to her knees and plead for mercy.

Aunt Poppy looked at her as if she'd painted the walls and floor black. "Why did you do this?"

Before Rilla could answer, her aunt reached for a wadded-up towel on the hamper. "And look what happened to your doll."

Aunt Poppy pulled the towel away. Chelsea, as stiff and lifeless as Summer, gazed at her with vacant eyes. At first Rilla thought the mermaid was playing possum, but then she knew.

The stars had shifted, breaking the lightning pattern.

The magic had ended. Her monsters were back to the state the M.O.T.M. Club had intended them to be.

"Isn't this one of those stuffed toys Abe Tamerow sent you?" Aunt Poppy asked. "From that club thing?"

Rilla nodded.

"Well, why'd you get her wet?" She gave Chelsea a good rubbing with the towel. "She's probably ruined now."

Rilla shrugged. "Maybe she jumped into the tub."

"Jumped?"

"I mean, *fell. Fell* into the tub."

"Excuse me, ladies." Dottie edged toward the door to avoid witnessing a family quarrel. "Lottie's waiting for me in the basement. We'll turn the water back on. Then you can drain the tub."

Aunt Poppy held Rilla's gaze with a bewildered look. "What does this mean, Rill? Are you okay?" She lifted her niece's hand. The one holding the can of tuna. "And what's this for?"

Rilla shrugged again. Often a shrug was the best kind of answer.

"Were you . . . playing? Like, make-believe? I mean, your mother told me you'd been playing with that toy the family from Cincinnati left behind."

Rilla flinched. *Thanks, Mom.*

Aunt Poppy fussed with Rilla's collar, straightening it. "You need to get out of the attic more and spend time with your friends. I think you're alone too much. It's not natural."

Shrug number three. *Agree with everything she says.*

"Aunt Poppy?" Rilla tried to look as apologetic as she could. "Would you mind not telling my mother? If I promise to clean the tub right now?"

"Puh," she said, borrowing Mother Lazuli's favorite expression.

Oh, yeah, the Earth sisters were angry at each other.

"Trust me," Aunt Poppy muttered. "I won't say a word to your mother." She tossed the wet mermaid to Rilla. "I just hope her stuffing isn't ruined."

"Sparrow isn't stuffed," Rilla teased.

Aunt Poppy laughed. "Sometimes I think she is."

"Thanks." Rilla stood on tiptoes to kiss her aunt on the cheek. An unexpected hug had worked on Sparrow; maybe an unexpected kiss would work on her aunt.

It did.

Smiling, she circled her niece in a hug. "You're a good kid," she whispered into Rilla's ear. "A little weird, but with a mother like Sparrow, what can we expect?"

Rilla agreed, wondering if Aunt Poppy saw herself as normal.

Aunt Poppy let go of her and sighed. "What a day. I need to go out to the barn and lift weights."

"No!" Rilla lunged between her aunt and the door.

Aunt Poppy looked at her as if the "weird verdict" was being confirmed right before her eyes. "Why not?"

"Maybe, um, you should help Sparrow this afternoon because Mother Lazuli isn't feeling well, and a *million* things have gone wrong, and—"

Aunt Poppy's eyebrows dipped suspiciously. "Did your mother tell you to ask me for help?"

"Nooooo." Rilla's brain whirred. She *had* to keep Aunt Poppy out of the barn. "It's just that *I* can't help her because I've got to clean the tub, then take the kittens to the vet."

Acting annoyed, Aunt Poppy faced the bathroom mirror and fluffed her hair. "Okay, okay. I'll help your mother first and lift weights later."

Yanking up a shirtsleeve, she flexed her biceps. "Look, Rill. I think the weights are definitely working."

Rilla agreed vigorously, accepting the invitation to squeeze her aunt's biceps. They felt more like mashed potatoes than muscles.

Aunt Poppy started down the attic steps.

"Wait." Rilla leaned out the door. "Can I ask you a question?"

"Shoot."

"Is José, um, your boyfriend?"

The question caught Aunt Poppy by surprise. Pausing, she gazed up at Rilla with a wide-eyed innocent look. "Is Joshua, um, *your* boyfriend?"

Double surprise.

"Touché." Rilla mimicked her aunt's innocent look, wishing she could answer, *"Yes, he is,"* and mean it. But that would involve Joshua Banks thinking of *her* as his girlfriend. Too complicated.

Back in the attic, Rilla locked the door—to prevent

Lottie from flying in to bawl her out after Dottie told her the "nightmare in the tub" tale.

Rilla drained the bath, stuffed damp greenery into garbage bags, and stacked wet rocks into one corner so she could carry them outside a few at a time.

Then she scoured the tub until it shone. Until there was no hint that a frisky mermaid from Aruba once lived and played there.

The vigorous work kept Rilla from crying over the whole thing.

But Chelsea could come to life again. All the monsters could.

That's right. Rilla smiled as she rinsed the tub. Knowing the legend was true made the lump in her throat disappear.

A few beads slipped down the drain before Rilla could catch them. Someday the Tonkawa sisters might discover a handful of coppery beads clogging the Harmony House septic tank and wonder how they got there.

Oh, well.

Sitting on the bed, Rilla wrapped the wet mermaid in a towel and cuddled her. Poor Chelsea. No more swimming. No more singing.

The mer-monster's hair was half braided, as though the magic had broken right in the middle of a braiding session.

"I'll finish it for you," Rilla promised. "I'll even buy new colored beads that go better with green hair." She smoothed Chelsea's damp locks. "How about wooden ones?"

Sounds of running footsteps clunked up the stairs. *Now* who?

Rilla tensed. *Please don't let it be Lottie. Or Sparrow.*

Someone banged frantically at the door.

Feeling curious, worried, and reluctant all at the same time, Rilla set Chelsea aside and trudged to open the door.

A white-faced Joshua Banks, clutching a lumpy pillowcase, burst into the attic. "Oh, Earth! Something terrible's happened!"

Joshua looked as if he was about to cry. "I-I've *killed* him!"

He shoved the limp pillowcase into Rilla's arms.

"Burly is . . . is dead!"

24
MAGIC IS HARD TO SECOND-GUESS

Joshua's gaze fell upon Chelsea, whose wet, tangly hair was bleeding green dye onto the white towel.

"I-Is that the mermaid? Is she . . . ?"

"Dead?" Rilla knew she shouldn't tease when her one true love was white from shock. "They're not exactly dead," she told him. "Remember when I read you the 'Legend of the Global Monsters'?"

He nodded.

"The legend calls the monsters *cozy collectibles*. That's all anybody thinks they are. But *we* know the legend is true."

"You mean, the part about stars lining up a certain way? Making the monsters come to life?"

"Yes."

The color flooded back into Joshua's face. "So what happened? Did the stars shift?"

"I guess. Maybe the earth's rotation has something to do with it too."

Rilla loved the way he was hanging on her every word.

Joshua pulled Burly from the pillowcase and set the torn and tattered monster on the bed.

Rilla's heart turned over at the sight of the silent May monster.

She reached for him. His ripped, dirty shirt reminded her of his wild spree in Willow Park. Now that she didn't have to buy monster food anymore, she could afford to stop by Soozi's Sporting Goods and buy him a new rugby shirt. He'd probably wear toddler size.

Joshua awkwardly folded the pillowcase. "Do you think the president of the Monster of the Month Club knows the legend is true?"

Rilla had wondered the same thing. Yet if anyone knew—especially a grown-up—the news would probably be splashed all over the pages of every newspaper in the country.

"No," she told him, feeling sure of her hunch. "I think you and I may be the only ones who know."

Joshua sat on the floor next to the bed. "If the monsters come from all over the world, wouldn't star patterns be different over each country?"

"I thought about that." Rilla straightened the ribbon holding Burly's whistle. "I even looked at the world atlas in my classroom. Aruba is due north of Argentina.

They fall along the same longitude. Maybe star patterns above those countries are similar."

"Oh."

"I'm just guessing, though. I still haven't figured out why the monsters from Botswana and New Zealand were alive at the same time."

Joshua was looking to her for answers she didn't have. "Magic is hard to second-guess," she told him.

Setting Burly aside, Rilla reached into her pile of pillow animals and pulled out a blue bird. "Would you like to meet the June monster?"

"Wow." Joshua touched the bird's soft fur. "Did it arrive dead? I mean . . ." He stopped to correct himself. "Stuffed?"

"Yes." Rilla showed him the June Selection card.

He studied it, then glanced at her. Disappointment crinkled his face. "Seeing the bird alive would have been really cool."

She agreed. "Well, the monsters have come alive twice this year. Maybe it will happen again. Who knows?"

You're being awfully calm about the whole thing, her mind told her. *And about the way Joshua is staring at you with that cute frown of his.*

Suddenly she didn't feel quite so nonchalant. Joshua had no further excuses to stop by the B & B. "Um, is Taco all right?" she asked.

"I think so. I found him snuggled up next to Burly.

He seemed confused about his master not moving or talking to him."

Rilla wondered if dogs were as smart as monsters.

"I brought Taco some dog food and a bowl for water. After he ate, he wanted to play, so I think he's going to be fine."

"Great. Thanks." Maybe Joshua would still come by—to play with the dog.

"Oh, no!" Rilla bounded off the bed. "I just remembered. My aunt's going to use the weight machine in the barn this afternoon. Could you take Taco to the park so she doesn't find him?"

"Sure." Joshua scrambled to his feet, as if eager to be off on another secret mission. "I'll go get him right now."

Burly's soccer ball was on the rug next to the bed. Picking it up, Joshua tossed it to Rilla. "Why don't you come with us?"

Her heart soared.

Then she remembered her promise to Sparrow. "Maybe later. I have to work for my mom this summer in exchange for keeping the kittens and getting them, um, fixed." *Why was that so hard to say in front of Joshua?* "I'm taking them to the vet this afternoon," she added.

"Wow. Handling three cats will be hard," Joshua said. "Can I help?"

"What about Taco?"

Joshua reached to touch Chelsea, gingerly, as if he expected her to flip her tail in greeting. "Don't you think the vet should take a look at the dog too? I mean, if you're going to keep him, he needs to get his shots."

"But I don't have enough—"

"I'll loan you the money. You can pay me back sometime."

They smiled at each other.

"Thanks," Rilla said.

Joshua picked up Burly one last time. With a sad look, he placed the sports monster between Chelsea and Summer. Taking the soccer ball from Rilla, he shoved it under Burly's arm. "See ya, buddy."

Glancing at Rilla, he acted embarrassed. "I'll go get Taco and wait for you at the end of the alley."

After Joshua left, Rilla sat on the bed for a long moment. She and Joshua Banks had plans for the summer.

Plans that didn't revolve around monsters.

Maybe he likes you.

You mean, the way I like him?

Suddenly Rilla felt the urge to write something profound in her journal. Yanking open the dresser drawer, she reached for the cookie tin.

Wait a minute.

"Why *write* what I'd like to say to Joshua?" she asked herself. "Why don't I just *say* it to him?"

Closing the drawer, she hurried outside to meet him.

25

POWERS PUT TO THE TEST

After dinner, Rilla worked on her herb book.

She'd come up with a few more ailments she wanted to find natural remedies for, like the flu, stuffy noses, coughs, and sunburn.

She was far from being finished. Illustrations still needed to be sketched. She still had to illustrate the book with colored pencils, but that might be fun. Then she had to fold pages for the inside and make a cover out of cardboard. After that, she'd cover the cardboard with leftover scraps of wallpaper from the green hall. Its herbal flower pattern would be perfect.

While she worked, she thought about her afternoon at the vet. It was fun. Well, more fun for her and Joshua than the poor kittens getting "fixed."

The doctor had given Taco a clean bill of health, then put out a citywide notice about the stray on her computer. She would board Taco for seventy-two hours, and if no one claimed him, he'd get all his shots and become an official Earth dog.

It was going to be a long seventy-two hours.

Rilla was *not* looking forward to breaking the *"Guess what? We have a dog!"* news to Sparrow. She'd have a lot to say about "another mouth to feed," but she was bound to be impressed that her daughter had acted so responsibly with the stray dog. Sparrow was big on responsibility.

Footsteps echoed on the attic stairs.

"Geez," Rilla grumbled. "Who is it *this* time?"

No one *ever* came to the attic—not since the Earth family first moved in. Yet over the past few days, the attic seemed to be Harmony House's most popular room.

Rilla had nothing to hide anymore, so she swung the door wide open and squinted into the darkness.

A massive turquoise form loomed in the stairwell.

Mother Lazuli? Spying again?

The woman swished past Rilla into the attic, flustered at being caught snooping. "Well, child, I just came to, uh, say good-bye."

"Good-bye? Are you leaving?" Rilla's heart leaped in ecstasy. She hoped the woman couldn't sense her overwhelming joy.

"I *must* leave." Mother Lazuli spoke with great dramatic flair. Lifting her chin like a bloodhound tracking a scent, she began to move around the attic, following her nose—stopping every few steps to touch Rilla's things.

"Are . . . are you looking for something?" Times like this, Rilla was glad her monsters were the nonliving kind.

"Leave I must."

Why the drama? You already said that.

"Harmony House is making me . . . quite ill."

"It is?" Rilla swallowed a laugh and tried to look concerned.

Mother Lazuli ran her fingertips along the windowsill as she toured the room.

"My afflicted feelings might have something to do with the approach of the summer solstice," she explained. "My powers are always put to the test then. Movements of stars and planets can cause strange things to happen."

Twirling to face Rilla, she watched for a reaction. "Don't you agree?"

Rilla's insides began to hip-hop. *Did the woman know?*

"I-I guess."

Mother Lazuli snatched Chelsea off the bed. "Why is this toy damp?"

"She, um, fell into the bathtub," Rilla answered.

The woman's eyes lasered through Rilla's skull, as if attempting to read her true thoughts.

Rilla forced her mind *not* to think about monsters. Instead, she pictured her herbal remedy book.

Mother Lazuli snorted. "Dedicated the book to your father, huh?"

Rilla's eyes cut to the pages on her desk. The dedication page was on top, but Mother L. was clear across the room.

Had she read the page when she entered the attic? Or was this her way of telling Rilla that she *could* read minds?

Yikes.

The woman pivoted, squinting into each dark corner. "The energy causing my afflictions has been drifting down to the first floor from this attic. Something in here is . . . is breaking harmony with the universe."

Double yikes.

She faced Rilla, looking like a turquoise tiger ready to pounce. "What is it, child?"

Rilla began to fiddle with the radio. "Ya got me," was all she said.

A shadow darkened the woman's face. She placed two fingers against her right temple. Was she picking up star signals? Or was the attic's *disharmonious energy* giving her a royal headache?

"Maybe you should take some feverfew," Rilla suggested in a polite voice. "For your head."

"Puh." The woman scowled at her. "A patient needn't prescribe medicine to the doctor."

"Sorry, ma'am."

Mother Lazuli finished her tour of the room, still clutching Chelsea. As she moved, she picked up two other items: Burly and Summer.

The hip-hop inside Rilla began again. *She knows.*

She knows what?

She knows it was the monsters who broke harmony with the universe. She knows they're not normal stuffed toys. Why else would she be drawn to those three out of everything else in the room?

Mother Lazuli set the monsters on the pillow with the other stuffed animals, but her narrowed eyes never wavered from Rilla's face.

She's waiting for you to confess.

Let her wait. I'll outlive her.

The staring match continued until the woman's attention was drawn toward the bathroom. Moving slowly, she opened the door and peeked in.

Rilla was enormously glad she'd emptied and scoured the tub. All Mother L. saw was a normal-looking bath— except for the pile of wet rocks in one corner. They held the psychic's attention for several long, puzzled moments.

Rilla closed her eyes. *Please go.* She didn't care if Mother L. picked up *that* thought. When she opened her eyes, a slight movement on the bed caught her attention.

Rilla gawked at her stuffed animal collection. Something had moved. But what?

Mother Lazuli emerged from the bathroom, lifting her chin again as though her prophetic gift was centered solely in her nostrils.

"Come," she said, spreading her turquoise arms. "Give Mother a good-bye hug."

Rilla moved to the door, turning so the woman's back was to the bed.

Just in case.

Reluctantly she hugged the woman.

Over Mother L.'s massive shoulder, Rilla's eye caught another movement—the slow spreading of sky blue wings.

She gasped.

"What's wrong?"

"Um." Rilla pulled away. "You hugged me too tight."

Mother Lazuli glowered, as if she knew Rilla was lying.

The woman blocked her view of the bed. Rilla stepped to one side, trying not to act suspicious. The newest monster moved awkwardly, like a baby bird trying its wings for the first time.

Mother L. grasped Rilla's chin. "Be good this summer," she ordered. "And help your mother."

The blue monster lifted a fuzzy head and craned her thin neck, slowly becoming aware of her surroundings.

"What's wrong?" Mother Lazuli would *not* let go of Rilla's chin.

"Nothing." She yanked away from the woman's iron

grip. *Go away!* her mind screamed at the snoopy sooth-sayer.

Mother Lazuli began to turn around.

Rilla grabbed her, sweeping her arms around the woman's neck, forcing another hug. "Oh, Mother Lazuli, I'm going to miss you," she fibbed.

Now the bird was twisting her head this way and that, looking for a place to fly.

Rilla jerked open the door and "helped" Mother L. from the attic. As gently as possible.

"What are you doing?" the woman shrieked indignantly.

"Oh, Mother, I don't want you to get any sicker by spending one extra second here in my afflicted attic."

Rilla cocked the door so the woman couldn't see the bed. Or the bird. "Come back again," she fudged. "Real soon."

Mother Lazuli's eyes were pools of fury. She started to lean around the door.

"Good trip home," Rilla chirped. "Say hello to Plum." Slamming the door, she locked it with a quick twist of her wrist.

CHEEP! CHEEP! SQUA-A-A-WK!

Rilla flinched as Mother Lazuli pounded on the door.

Psychic or not, everyone within fifty feet heard the mysterious cry of Rilla's monster bird.

26

HOW I SPENT MY SUMMER VACATION

"Child!" shouted Mother Lazuli. "What was *that*?"

Rilla thought it best not to answer.

After a few minutes of near indecipherable grumblings and threats, the Oracle of Harmony House gave up and clomped down the steps. The last words Rilla caught were "misbehaved child" and "too much of a bother."

Vastly relieved, Rilla tiptoed toward the bed, scrutinizing the June monster, who had suddenly sprung to life.

It was eyeing her intently. Looking for dinner?

Rilla hoped she didn't look like a tall, skinny worm. An *Earth*worm—ha!

"Welcome to Harmony House," she cooed.

The bird clucked an answer.

Rilla reached out warily to lift Summer off the bed.

The monster reared back, spread her wings, and rose into the air.

"Wow," Rilla gasped, watching as the bird dipped to avoid hitting the ceiling fan.

The attic didn't offer much room for a flying monster. Still, the bird circled once, then flitted in and out of the bathroom. Her fur wings made a pleasant fluttery sound.

Gliding to a stop on top of the bookcase, Summer peered down at her with one eye.

Thrilled, Rilla clapped for the graceful bird. Should she call Joshua and tell him the news? Tell him to come right over and meet the June monster?

No. There'd be time for that tomorrow. When they met at the animal clinic to visit Taco and pick up the kittens.

Preening her fur, the bird remained on the bookcase, clucking and scolding. Was she thinking of building a nest?

"I'll help," Rilla told her, already planning to collect twigs from the yard.

What if she lays eggs and hatches blue baby monster birds?

I'd be a grandmother! Rilla laughed at the absurd idea.

Stashing the June Selection card in the cookie tin, she put on her pajamas—the ones Sparrow hated because of the logo: *Whirled Peas.* Rilla thought it was hilarious.

She moved her stuffed animal collection to the chair, choosing Burly for a bedmate. (Chelsea's hair was still too damp.)

Should she feed the bird monster? She didn't have cola in the attic, or worms (thank heavens). But she did have some of Sparrow's organic sunflower seeds in her desk. Finding them, she scattered a handful on top of the dresser.

Rilla climbed into bed, leaving the light on to watch Summer, hunched near the ceiling like a cotton candy vulture.

Hugging Burly, Rilla silently thanked him for bringing her and Joshua Banks together.

Another month, another monster. More trouble, more secrets.

Ah, but she's so nifty.

All of them are nifty. And demanding, noisy, perpetually hungry . . .

"I know," Rilla said out loud. "Still, she needs me."

Summer spotted the sunflower seeds. Leaping off the bookcase, she fluttered to the dresser and pecked at them until they were gone.

Then, spreading her yellow claws, she fluffed her feathery fur and settled in, ready to perch for the night.

Rilla clicked off the lamp.

"Good night, Summer," she whispered, wondering what type of traumas her newest monster would bring. Smooth sailing obviously wasn't in the stars for her year of good fortune, promised by the monster legend.

Count your blessings, not your sorrows.

A teaching from one of Sparrow's mugs. Still, it was good advice, so Rilla lay in the dark and counted her blessings:

- Mother Lazuli will be long gone by morning.

- The kittens are mine to keep.

- With luck, I'll soon have a dog, too.

- The ugly scabs on my knees are healing.

- I have another live monster with which to impress my one true love.

- I'm getting to "know" my family—finally.

The last blessing stopped her. Was Sparrow right? Had her father really come looking for her?

Well, why not help him? Why couldn't she search for *him*?

The idea thrilled her and chilled her at the same time.

Ms. Noir at the library could help. And it would be a summer project she would *really* enjoy. After she finished her herbal remedy book.

Rilla closed her eyes to sleep, imagining the true essay she'd write for Sparrow when the home-schoolers started meeting again in the fall:

How I Spent My Summer Vacation
or
Monsters and My One True Love

Rilla couldn't *wait* to find out how the essay ended.

EARTH'S HERBAL REMEDIES
～ AND HOME CURES ～
by Rilla Harmony Earth

MINOR CUTS AND SCRAPES

Aloe Vera:

Aloe Vera is known as "the first-aid plant."
Break off one of the plant's thick, fleshy
leaves and squeeze its clear gel onto the
wound. The gel stops pain, reduces the
chance of infection, and promotes healing.

Bistort:

Bistort is a natural antiseptic. It is one of
the strongest herbal astringents.
Apply the powdered root to a wound to
stop bleeding.

STOMACHACHES

Peppermint:

Tea made from peppermint leaves acts
as a sedative to the stomach and aids
in digestion.

Ginger:

Ginger in many forms helps to settle an

upset stomach. To make soothing ginger tea, add two teaspoons of grated gingerroot per cup of boiling water. Steep for ten minutes.

HEADACHES

Feverfew:

Feverfew is a natural pain reliever. To relieve a headache, chew two fresh leaves, or take a capsule filled with the powdered leaf.

White Willow Bark:

White willow bark works like aspirin; in fact, aspirin was created from a chemical which is found in white willow bark called salicin.
For headaches, soak one teaspoon of powdered bark in a cup of cold water for eight hours. Strain. Add honey and lemon to taste.

COLDS

Golden Seal:

This herb stimulates the immune system to fight infections and kill germs. Steep 1/2 teaspoon of the powdered root in hot water, then add honey to sweeten its bitter taste.

Garlic:

Garlic has been called "nature's antibiotic." This "stinking rose" is the world's second-oldest medicine. Garlic can be taken in odor-free capsules or the crushed cloves can be used to season food.

HICCUPS

Granulated sugar is believed to relieve hiccups: eat a spoonful. Chewing on dry bread also helps. Other home remedies include sucking on crushed ice or slurping orange juice.

About the Author

Rilla Harmony Earth lives in Harmony House Bed and Breakfast. She is thirteen years old, likes bicycling, reading, watching old movies, and taking care of her extensive stuffed animal collection.

This is her first book.

Sparrow's books:

Back to Eden by Jethro Kloss (Back to Eden Books, 1939).

The Complete Woman's Herbal by Anne McIntyre (Henry Holt, 1994).

The Healing Herbs by Michael Castleman (Rodale Press, 1991).

Herbally Yours by Penny C. Royal (Sound Nutrition, 1976).

Prevention's Book of Home Remedies (Rodale Press, 1990).

Today's Herbal Health by Louise Tenney (Woodland Books, 1992).

NOTE: Herbal remedies have been used for thousands of years. Those listed here are intended to offer historical usage only, and are not meant as a prescription for self treatment. A doctor should always be consulted.